ROTATION
PLAN

The Killing Trail

The notorious Dylan brothers are riding high until they pick a fight with the wrong man, a drifter called Jared Carter, who leaves three of the brothers dead in the street.

The youngest remaining brother, Nat Dylan, vows to find Carter and avenge his brothers, but he soon finds that things are not as simple as they seem. . . .

As Nat learns more about Carter, he realizes that his quest for revenge is unjust, but honor still demands that he avenge his family.

Can Nat survive a gunfight with the man who single-handedly killed his three brothers, or will his sense of honor be his downfall?

ISBN 978-0-7090-8898-1

Robert Hale Limited
Clerkenwell House
Clerkenwell Green
London EC1R 0HT

www.halebooks.com

Typeset by
Derek Doyle & Associates, Shaw Heath
Printed and bound in Great Britain by
CPI Antony Rowe, Chippenham and Eastbourne

The Killing Trail

Chuck Tyrell

A Black Horse Western

ROBERT HALE · LONDON

CHAPTER ONE

Alton Jackson sat hunkered on his heels, staring into the campfire. Damn! Damn! Damn! A trip all the way from Longhorn to get a herd from the Snyder gang, only for those tough men to say no cattle were available. They'd said he could get those cows for ten cents on the dollar. Then they said none were available. Maybe next spring, they said. Jackson needed those cattle to make the Wagonwheel respectable.

And damn that drifter. What was his name? Jared Carter. That brought to mind another drifter, a man named Havelock, who stood up for one of his boys who'd taken a lashing and then run. Damn that boy! Hadn't he been provided with a roof over his head and food to eat? So he'd been chastised. Children need chastisement if they were to grow into responsible adults.

Jackson grimaced at the memory of chastisement he'd received at the hand of his stern father. But then, that pain had made him what he was – a

5

respected man in the community, with even better things to come. He had it all planned out. The next step, wed Carmen Vasquez.

He threw the Arbuckles' grounds in the bottom of his cup into the fire; it hissed and flared. His mind went back to the drifter. He didn't like to back down from any man, but there had been death in that drifter's eyes. Jackson shivered involuntarily as he reached for the coffee pot. Two days would put them in Horsehead, and then Longhorn would be only a long day's ride away. Jackson wished he were already there. He smiled at the thought of all he planned for Longhorn – first the town, then Alchesay County. With the note he held on the Double Diamond, he'd soon have that spread, and after marriage to Carmen, the Vasquez land grant would be as good as his, too. Jackson chuckled aloud.

Frenchy Durand assigned the watches for the night. Jackson trusted the big man to run things on the trail. Durand, a rawhide-tough man, took care of expeditions like this one. All Jackson had to do was ride. He slept well with Durand in charge.

Durand placed the camp deep in Boneyard Canyon, so the rising sun painted the sheer sides crimson long before it ever touched the sandy bottom. Breakfast of sowbelly and frybread was over soon after the sky turned blue with the dawn. The six men had just mounted when shots rang out.

Breathing stopped as six pairs of eyes searched the heights for sign of gunsmoke. There was none. Then six more shots, evenly spaced and deliberate-sounding. Echoing in the canyon made it hard to locate the source of the shooting, but Durand nodded south, upstream.

The group moved slowly down the trail, Winchesters across the bows of their saddles. A third volley of shots came. Then a fourth.

They found a camp, but no one was there. The fire was scattered and stomped dead, covered with damp sand. The tracks said five horses had left not long before. Down by the river they found a well-punctured tin can – the shots they'd heard were someone practicing.

Half an hour later, the horse tracks veered toward a trail out of the canyon.

'Reckon they're riding the mesa to Horsehead,' Durand said. He led Jackson's men up the same trail. They topped out about noon and saw dust raised by the other party a good hour ahead.

The camp was dry that night, but Jackson knew they'd be in Horsehead the next day where he could get a decent meal at Grannie Alda's and a good drink at the Bucket of Blood. Shortly after they'd saddled up, a series of shots came from up ahead. Later they found a fruit can shattered by bullets until it hardly looked like a can at all. 'We've gained a few minutes on them,' Durand said. 'Likely they'll still be in Horsehead when we get there.'

When the sun was high, Durand had Jackson and his riders dismount and wet their bandannas with water from their canteens and wipe out their horses' mouths. Horsehead and the Radito River were still four or five hours away.

They tromped across red clay and broken sandstone for nearly an hour before Durand let them mount. Even then, they kept the horses at a walk. Still, the sun was almost down when they topped the bluff north of Horsehead. The Twenty-Four ranch house stood on the bluff, whitewashed and fronted by plank-fenced paddocks. Jackson noticed everything was in perfect repair. *This is how the Wagonwheel will look when I get the land and cattle I need,* he thought.

Durand took them to Horsehead Crossing on the Radito to water the horses. Then they rode single file up Main Street to Bigelow's Livery.

'Howdy, Frenchy,' said Sam Bigelow. 'Staying long?'

Durand shot a quick glance at Jackson, then shook his head. 'We'll be headed for Longhorn in the morning,' he said. 'Anyone in town?'

'Cal Tyler and his bunch came in about an hour ago. He's going to Longhorn, too. He had an extra man with him. Don't know for sure, but the way he wears his gun back behind his right hip makes me think it might be Nat Dylan.'

'Who's Nat Dylan?' Jackson wanted to know.

'He's the youngest of the Dylan brothers. The other three caught lead in Ouray, what was it, four, five years ago? Jared Carter shot 'em. Heard Dylan was gunning for Carter.'

Jackson's ears perked when Bigelow said Dylan was

after Jared Carter, because that was the name of the drifter who'd stood him off in the desert. 'Dylan's here?'

'Well, I think that was him,' Bigelow said.

'He's one to steer clear of, boss,' said Durand. 'He's quick. Quick to pull his hogleg. Quick to pull the trigger. And I ain't heard nothing about him missing what he shoots at.'

Horses stabled and cared for, Jackson gave each man a gold eagle and warned them of an early morning start. He knew Durand would rouse them, because the big man was a teetotaler, and he wasn't even a Mormon.

After venison, beans, and sourdough bread at Grannie Alda's, Jackson pushed through the swinging doors of the Bucket of Blood. At the middle of the bar, he ordered whiskey and a cigar. He tipped his white hat back on his head and tossed back the whiskey, smiling as the warmth spread through his body. He cut the end of the cigar off with his pocketknife. He licked the whole cigar well, and began lighting it with a lucifer from a box on the bar. As he lit the stogie, his eyes swept the bar's patrons.

A blond man dressed in black played poker with three cowboys. He was deadpan and motionless, but gave the impression of being wound tight as a watch spring.

Another man at the end of the bar caught Jackson's attention. He stood with his left arm on the bar. He wore his gun on the right side, almost in the small of his back, and tilted so the grip was ready if he swept his hand back, palm open and thumb to the body.

Jackson puffed his cigar, quaffed a second drink, and walked over to the man, who watched him come with a raised eyebrow.

'My name is Colonel Alton Jackson. I own the Wagonwheel Outfit in Longhorn. I assume you are Nat Dylan.'

The man nodded. 'I am.'

'Would you like a job?'

'Doing what?'

'I need a man killed,' Jackson said.

'I'm not a killer,' Dylan said, 'so I reckon you're talking to the wrong man.'

CHAPTER TWO

Nat Dylan stayed in Horsehead when Cal Tyler and his men rode on. He liked the Bucket of Blood, and Horsehead seemed an interesting town. True, he'd shot a card shark in Jackson's Hole, but the gambler deserved shooting, though Dylan rode out three steps ahead of the sheriff. He'd talked to the law in Horsehead and Marshal Rencher didn't have any flyers from Wyoming.

Dylan stood at the bar in his usual position. With his empty whiskey glass at his elbow, he watched a quiet card game at the back table.

'Will ye be wanting another, sor?' The barman was an old soldier with a ramrod back despite his generous belly and keen ice-blue eyes that could twinkle at a good joke or spark with indignation when cowboys went beyond common sense in their drunken revelry. Dylan knew of the sawed-off shotgun behind the counter and no doubt Delaney could use the weapon well. He nodded.

Delaney poured him a generous two fingers from

the good whiskey bottle in the hutch.

The killing job Alton Jackson offered held no appeal. The colonel didn't even know where Carter was, except to say he was seen heading south from Mexican Hat. Still, he'd have to do something soon or he'd be out of drinking money and forced to live on free lunch at the bar or ride the chuck line.

Dylan preferred towns. He was born in Silver City and had gone from one town to the next until Ouray.

Back then, he was the littlest Dylan, a kid wet behind the ears and hanging to the coat-tails of his big brothers. Still, he'd never forget that day in Ouray.

Actually, Nat Dylan was deeply in love. His brothers insisted that he attend school, where he was the oldest student, if not the biggest. But that didn't matter. He was in love with Miss Rebecca Shoemeister and his eyes followed her as she taught sums to the younger students. He dwelt on every word she spoke and he did every homework assignment with unfailing diligence.

Shig and Miles, older than Nat by a dozen years, saw his infatuation and teased him unmercifully.

'But she's only nineteen,' Nat argued, 'and I'm almost fifteen. Lots of folks got wives as older than they are. Just look at the Swensens at the bakery. I bet a dime to a dollar the Dane's younger than his stringbean wife. So what's wrong if I'm sweet on Miss Shoemeister?'

His brothers laughed.

Nat liked story time best of all, because Miss

Shoemeister read aloud in her melodic contralto voice. At story time, Nat learned of knights and chivalry and how a man should throw his coat in the mud so a lady could step on it and not dirty her slippers.

He sometimes saw himself as the knightly gentleman and Rebecca as the noble maidenly lady, and he wished for a puddle to throw his coat over so she could step on it. Sometimes when she bent over a young scholar to guide a hand or give a word of encouragement, the sun would catch the stray hairs at the nape of her neck and turn them into burnished gold. In those moments, Nat Dylan loved Rebecca Shoemeister so much it felt as if his heart might stop.

On the unforgettable day, Marshal Flint came looking for Nat long before the end of the school day. He stuck his grizzled gray head through the door and stood there until Miss Shoemeister noticed him.

'Yes, Marshal?'

'I come for Nat Dylan, Miss.'

'Mr Dylan is at his studies.'

'Sorry, miss. This is important. Could I see you outside for a moment?'

Miss Shoemeister stepped out for a moment, then came back in. She walked to Dylan's seat on the back row and laid her hand gently on his shoulder. He found it very hard to breathe.

'Mr Dylan. Something important has happened down in town. Could you go with Marshal Flint?

Please.' Her eyes looked very sad and Dylan wondered why, but he couldn't refuse the woman he loved.

'Yes, Miss Shoemeister,' he said properly. 'I'll go with him right away.' How he'd practiced so he could speak to her correctly.

Dylan grabbed his hat and rushed outside. The marshal stood first on one foot and then the other.

'Come on, son,' he said gruffly. 'This ain't gonna be pleasant.' The marshal swung up on his big bay horse and waited for Dylan to follow on his mouse-colored mustang.

'What's happened, Marshal?'

'You'll find out soon enough.' The marshal turned his horse toward town. By the time they got there, a crowd had gathered. Dylan and the marshal used their horses to shoulder through the people. There, Dylan saw the still forms of his brothers.

'Miles! Dave! Shig!' Dylan piled off his mustang and ran to Miles, big Miles, giant Miles, now just a lump of dead flesh lying in a pool of blood on the hotel porch.

Strangely, Dylan's eyes were dry. Next he inspected Shig. Then Dave. Dead. Three brothers. Dead. Dylan turned to the marshal. 'Only my brothers are dead, marshal. No one else. Who did it? Who killed my kin?'

'Miles had a run-in with a drifter earlier, son. Told him to get outta town. The man buffaloed Miles and went to get some sleep at the hotel. Your brothers came after him and got the raw end of the deal, though it looks like he caught lead.'

'The drifter have a name?'

'Barkeep said the name was Jared Carter.'

Dylan tried the name on his tongue. 'Jared Carter.' It had a bitter taste.

The undertaker came. 'Want I should take care of the deceased?' he asked.

Dylan stared at him for a moment. Then nodded. 'See they're done for proper, if you would.' He walked over to Shig, the skinny Dylan brother, and carefully removed his gunbelt. Shig's Remington was lying in the dirt of the street. The dead man's bloody prints covered the grip and hammer. Dylan cinched the belt around his waist, then picked up the pistol and shoved it in the holster. He'd clean the gun later.

'You can take the other hardware to the house, Marshal. We'll bury my brothers in the morning.'

Nat Dylan cleaned the Remington Army .45 carefully that night. And he rolled the killer's name over on his tongue. Jared Carter. 'It'll be a year or two or five, who knows,' he said aloud, 'but some day you'll turn around, Jared Carter, and I'll be standing there with this gun in my hand, I promise.'

Nat Dylan mounted Bronc with the fresh-cleaned Remington in his holster and a box of .45 ammunition in his saddle-bags. Not a day passed but that he rode out to Latigo Wash east of Horsehead to practice drawing and shooting. He figured he must have fired more than a hundred, maybe two hundred boxes of shells through that walnut-

15

handled Remington he took from Shig's body. He'd messed around with the positioning of his holster. Tried it right and left. He found he didn't like the forward position on the left hip, and carrying it on his right thigh was a bother. Finally he arrived on a system where the gun was fitted in a holster that rode aslant the cartridge belt almost in the small of his back. Putting his thumb on his hip with the hand open to the rear brought the grip to hand. The rest was pulling the Colt while thumbing back the hammer, pointing it like a finger, and gently squeezing the trigger until the hammer fell and the cartridge exploded. These days it was unusual not to hit what he was looking at.

Down in the bottom of the wash, he got off Bronc and tied him to a nearby willow. He pulled a bottle from the saddle-bags and drained the last two swallows of whiskey from it. He took fifty strides down the sandy bottom of the wash and set the bottle on a waist-high outcropping.

Back where Bronc was tied, Dylan fished the box of cartridges from the saddle-bags and put them on a large rock near the far bank. This far away, he wouldn't upset Bronc, not that he was gun-shy.

For nearly half an hour, Dylan practiced sweeping his hand back, grasping the Colt, and bringing it into line. Somewhere he'd heard that the body remembers moves repeated often in exactly the same way, so he made sure he drew the weapon with the same smooth movement time after time.

Nat Dylan did not consider himself a gunfighter or

a shootist, but five years before he'd sworn revenge. He'd vowed to kill the man who'd taken his family away, and he knew the time would come when he'd need to get the Remington out fast and shoot straight.

Dylan pulled the .45 with a flowing motion, thumbing back the hammer as the gun came up, and squeezing off a shot as it came into line. The neck of the whiskey bottle disappeared.

He replaced the weapon and repeated the draw and fire. When the bottle was shattered beyond use as a target, Dylan stood a piece of driftwood up against the wall and kept at his practice. Fifty times he pulled the trigger. Fifty times the bullet hit the target. He used the last five cartridges in the box to load the Remington. He'd clean it back in Horsehead.

When he mounted Bronc, he noticed a stocky man on a dark brown horse watching from the lip of a mesa nearly half a mile away. He sat with both hands on the saddle horn. The man wore an unusual Buscadero gunbelt with the pistol on his left side, butt forward.

He took his horse over the edge of the mesa in a skittering slide to the bank of the wash. Somehow the brown horse seemed in perfect control during the wild descent. Dylan waited quietly for the man to approach. He pulled up far away enough not to be a threat, but close enough to talk.

'You're right handy with that weapon, son.' The stocky man spoke first.

'I practice some.'

'Pays.'

The two men sat their horses in silence. Then the stranger spoke again. 'I'll be Vince Holly,' he said. 'Got me a bit of a ranch over at Fleming Seep and I wear a star now and again. I do enjoy good shooting, son, and you're better than most.'

'I'm Nat Dylan.'

Holly nodded gravely. 'Any relation to the Dylans in Ouray, Colorado?'

'Brother.'

The stocky man nodded again. 'Heard about the shooting,' he said in a soft drawl. 'Come to think of it, I seen Jared Carter two days ago.'

Dylan's head came up and his eyes focused intently on Holly's face.

He continued as if he didn't notice. 'Almost didn't recognize Carter. He wore jeans and a leather jacket, rode a long-legged mule, and led a grulla pony.'

Dylan's blood raced. Suddenly his mouth was full of saliva. His eyes glinted. 'Where d'ya think he was headed?'

'Well, his brother's got a spread on Bent Creek and his girlfriend lives at the Crossbow. Reckon he's going south. Was I him, I'd go to Longhorn and work from there, but then again, I ain't him.'

Dylan nodded grimly. Maybe he'd take that job Jackson offered after all. Though he didn't like the man.

'Mind if I take a pot at your target?' Holly snaked the Colt from his Buscadero and fired one shot at the driftwood. Then another. Both tore chunks from the already battered target.

'Like to keep my hand in,' Holly said with a tight smile. He slid the pistol back into its accustomed place. 'I know youngsters like you don't like to hear advice, but I suggest you think twice about hunting for Jared Carter. First, he's a hairy wolf from the high country. He won't kill easy. Second, he's a good man, and no good man deserves to die.'

'Jared Carter killed my brothers,' Dylan said through clenched teeth.

Holly gave him a long look. 'Way I heard it, there was three Dylans and one Carter. . . .' Holly reined his mount toward Horsehead and left Dylan to think about what he'd said.

Holly's parting words were still echoing in Dylan's mind when he gathered up his few belongings and set out for Longhorn, his .45 Remington freshly cleaned and fully loaded.

CHAPTER THREE

Nat Dylan didn't ride due south. He'd spent more than one night sleeping on the ground, and he preferred a roof over his head. He took the stage road to Sulphur Springs station, where he spent the first night. Then he turned south toward Grant's Crossing, where the freight road from Santa Fe crossed El Claro River.

A few miles outside Grant's Crossing, he came upon a freight train camped on the north side of the Yavapai River ford.

Dylan topped the rise north of the ford near sunset. He automatically put a palm to the butt of his Remington as he started down the slope toward the circles of Murphy wagons. He counted sixty-three of the five-ton monsters. The herd of oxen was to the east; looked to be some 500 head. Men crowded around the fires as cooks dished out food with huge ladles. Dylan could hear the sound of a smithy at work. Likely some of the oxen had thrown shoes. The wagon train was a community on wheels, except there were no women and children, and fewer than a dozen horses.

Dylan rode up to the nearest circle of wagons, the one closest to the ford. He reckoned maybe the wagon boss was there.

'Hello the camp,' he called when he got within shouting distance.

A man with a rifle answered. 'Come in easy, stranger, and keep your hands on the saddle horn.'

Dylan nudged Bronc ahead until he came up to the man on watch.

'Like to talk to the wagon boss,' he said.

The rifleman looked at him for a long time, then nodded. 'Get down, son. Ed Mott's the big man over there by the fire. You tie your roan to the wagon wheel there before you go in, y'hear.'

'Thanks,' Dylan said, and dismounted. He secured Bronc and walked into the circle. Heads turned as he approached the fire, but no one stopped eating.

Ed Mott was the biggest man Dylan had ever seen. At least six inches over six feet and built like a collection of casks and barrels. His entire face was covered with hair except for a huge bulb of a nose, a pair of ice-blue eyes, and a high forehead that looked like a target amidst all that wild hair.

Dylan walked over to the man mountain. 'Mr Mott,' he said, speaking loudly to be heard over the cacophony of the camp.

Mott stopped making entries in his tally book and looked up. He said nothing but his eyes questioned Dylan.

'My name's Nat Dylan, sir, and if you're headed for Longhorn, I'd like to tag along. I can pay for my keep.'

'Why'd you wanna go with us? You'd be in Longhorn tomorrow on a good horse, and you could spend tonight in the hotel at Grant's Crossing just down the trail. It'll take us three days.'

Dylan shrugged. 'Never seen a train like this. Thought it might be interesting.'

'You won't be seeing trains like this any more,' Mott said. 'The railroad has made hauling freight from Santa Fe a chancy thing. Not much money in it. Fact is, I reckon this'll just about be the last one for Ed Mott. Think I'll hitch horses to my Murphys and haul from Horsehead to Camp Kinishba instead.

'Be that what it may, you're welcome, young'un,' the wagon boss said. 'Bones! Get this boy a bait of beef and beans and whatever else you've got cooked up.'

A skinny scarecrow of a man in an apron three sizes too big brought a tin plate piled high with boiled beef, pinto beans, and saleratus biscuits. Dylan thanked him and dug in.

Finished, he put the tin plate and spoon in the tub at the cook wagon. He unsaddled Bronc and took him to water. He hobbled the horse so he could graze but wouldn't be tempted to wander off.

Dylan hadn't planned on sleeping out, so he had no bedroll. He'd make do with a saddle blanket on the ground, a saddle for his pillow, and his duster as a blanket. Wouldn't be the first time. He spread his things out beneath the Murphy wagon Mott told him to sleep under.

A half-dozen men had built a second fire on the other side of the circle of wagons. They were soon deep in a game of poker, laying their bets on a barrel-head. Dylan wandered over to watch.

Even in the dark, Dylan stood out. Where the freighters wore button-front shirts and canvas trousers, Dylan had a dark vest over a creamy linen shirt and dark, tightly-woven wool trousers. And instead of the round-crowned hats favored by the teamsters, Dylan wore a pearl-gray, square-crowned hat with a short, tightly curled brim. Dylan looked like a city man. Some might even think he was a dude in his clean-cut finery.

The freighters came in every shape and form: little men with big swaggers and big men with bigger egos. The card game was a noisy affair. Each card got a whoop of joy or a groan of disappointment. Winners danced jigs around the fire when they won a pot of pennies and nickels.

The cavorting gamblers brought a tight smile to Dylan's lips and he ran a hand over his day-old stubble, which was already a thick black shadow on his square-jawed face.

'Come join, slicker.' A freighter nearly double Dylan's bulk invited him, perhaps thinking the young man could be easily fleeced of his pocket change.

Dylan smiled and shook his head. His years in saloons since his brothers died had made his skills a match for any card shark west of the Mississippi.

'Come on,' the man urged. 'Figure maybe a little of our honest dirt will rub off on your fancy clothes?'

A hard look came into Dylan's eyes. 'You invite me in, bullwhack, and you'll lose everything you have,' he said.

The teamster laughed. 'You think you can take me, come along and try.'

Dylan stared at the man, then gave a short nod. The players made room for him on a log.

'Penny ante,' the dealer said, and started his deal. Dylan played with his customary deadpan expression, and slowly the pile of coins on the barrel-head in front of him grew. One by one the rowdy players quieted down, then dropped out. At last, only Dylan and the big man remained. The other freighters stood in a circle around the two men, watching every move. The big man crowed when he won a small pot. Dylan smiled his tight smile and dealt the next hand.

'Hit me,' the man said, holding up three fingers. Dylan gave him three new cards. The man grinned and put a dollar on the barrel-head. 'No more penny ante,' he said. Dylan nodded and matched the bet without even looking at his cards.

The pot grew to twenty dollars before Dylan even knew what he had in his hand. He glanced at them and said, 'I'll take two.'

The new cards gave him a dead man's hand – aces and eights. He left the cards face down on the barrelhead and stared at the big man across from him. Sweat beaded the man's brow, though the night was cool. He looked at the pot and back at his cards, then back at the pot again.

'I don't think you should raise,' Dylan said. 'You'll only lose more.'

The man licked his lips. He stared at the pot. He closed his eyes and turned his face to the heavens. 'I'll see your hand,' he finally said, and turned up his cards. He had three tens.

Dylan showed his cards – three aces and a pair of eights. He calmly collected the pot without even looking at the big bullwhacker. He stood up and shoved the coins in his pocket. 'Thanks for the entertainment,' he said, and turned to leave. He'd taken no more than half a dozen steps when the big man lunged to his feet.

'You cheat!' he screamed.

Dylan paused but didn't turn around.

'You cheat. I don't know how, but you do . . . you did. And I'll have my coin back.' He pulled a long Green River knife from the scabbard on his belt and took three pounding, running steps toward Dylan with the knife held kidney-high.

Dylan calmly palmed his Remington as he turned to meet the man's charge and shot him. The bullet plowed into the man's chest between the second button and his left shirt pocket, but his inertia carried him forward as he fell. He skidded across the ground until his face rested a scant two inches from Dylan's boots.

'I don't cheat,' Dylan said.

Ed Mott's roar came as the echo of Nat Dylan's

gunshot. The men stood frozen as the wagonmaster strode across the wagon circle. Mott held his hand out for Dylan's gun.

'Give me the hogleg.'

Dylan slowly shook his head. 'Meaning no disrespect, Mr Mott, but this is all I got to protect myself. An' you can see that Jehu was gonna carve me up with his toad sticker.'

'He won alla Red's money, Cap'n. An' Red figured he had to be cheating,' said a gray-haired teamster with streaks of white in his beard.

Mott fastened Dylan with hard blue eyes.

'I told them I'd win,' Dylan said. 'But they didn't believe me.' He returned Mott's stare. 'I don't cheat,' he said again.

After a long moment, Mott nodded. 'Self-defense,' he said, 'but I can't let you stay here tonight. Grant's Crossing's south across the ford. I'll have to ask you to ride out.'

Dylan holstered his Remington in answer. 'Sorry to have bothered you,' he said, and went to gather his things.

Bronc was not happy about being saddled again with only a couple of hours to graze. But once he'd waded the Yavapai River ford, he set off for Grant's Crossing at a ground-eating lope. Dylan gave no more thought to the red-headed bullwhacker. Instead, his thoughts raced ahead to Longhorn and the possibility of meeting Jared Carter gun to gun.

Bronc clopped across the Claro Bridge before midnight, and Dylan put the roan in the ramshackle livery stable at the end of the main street, paying four bits for a covered stall and two quarts of oats. Bronc had made good time; he deserved the feed.

Bartley's Saloon stood across the street from Bartley's Mercantile. Four other false-front buildings lined the street, but two were deserted. Their windows gaped, broken, and their paint peeled.

Grant's Crossing is skidding downhill, Dylan thought. His boots kicked up miniature dust devils all the way from the stable to the boardwalk that joined the six buildings. He paused in front of Bartley's, his saddle-bags over his shoulder. ROOMS, a sign in the window said. Two coal-oil lamps burned in the saloon. Inside, it was silent as death.

Dylan entered the vestibule and shouldered his way through the swinging door. It protested his passing with shrill squeaks. Not a customer sat at any of the six tables. The piano at the back of the room was covered and silent, but the bar was smooth from use and fresh-wiped. A gray-haired man in shirtsleeves and garters stood behind it, watching Dylan carefully. His face was held neutral, as if he felt that speaking would scare this valuable customer off.

Dylan put a hand on the bar. 'Good whiskey and your best room,' he said.

The gray man smiled, showing big gapped teeth. 'I'm right down to the bottom of my really good whiskey,' he said, pulling a bottle of Turley's Mill from under the bar. It was less than one-third full. He wiped a shot glass on his apron and filled it with amber liquor. He pushed the drink across the bar.

Dylan lifted the shot glass with two fingers and a thumb. 'Room?' he asked, then downed the whiskey in a single gulp, breathing deeply as it burned its way through his innards and into his bloodstream.

'Once they was women here,' the barman said with apology in his voice. 'The rooms was theirs. Now you can have your pick for a quarter. No entertainment, though.'

Dylan tapped the glass with his index finger. The barman filled it with the good whiskey. This time Dylan sipped. It was still good.

The barman rambled on about the town Grant's Crossing used to be. 'But once the railroad came, they was no use to haul freight from Santy Fe this way,' he said. 'And folks just kind of faded away. They's a few two-bit ranches around and that spread of Fenmore Dillard's, but young Shawn Brodie's in Yuma Prison and his ma, Widow Brodie, she went and married ol' Dillard.' The barman sighed. 'Them big wagon trains sure brought the money,' he said.

'Ed Mott's camped at the Yavapai River ford. Says it's his last trip,' Dylan said.

The barman lifted an eyebrow. 'You know Ed Mott?'

'We've met.'

'Well, I'm Bartley Witherspoon. I'm about all the business they is left in Grant's Crossing. I get by, but Mott quitting the run'll make it harder.'

'Nat Dylan.'

Bartley took a step back from the bar and his face took on a careful look.

28

'Dylan?'

'That's right.'

'Will the room be for one night, Mr Dylan?' He paused, and then in a small voice asked, 'Or will you be staying longer?'

'One night.'

'A quarter for the room and fifty cents for the Turley's Mill . . . if you don't mind.'

Dylan sensed he was being asked to go to his room. He finished the whiskey and put a silver dollar on the bar. 'Keep it,' he said, 'and give me the key to the room on the northeast corner.' From there he could see the Claro Bridge.

'Yessir. Thankee properly.'

Bartley gave him a brass key with FAITH stamped into it. 'That was her name,' he said. 'But they all went to Tombstone.'

Dylan smiled his tight smile, took the key, and climbed the well-worn stairs at the back of the saloon. The steps rose to intersect with the hallway that bisected the second floor and paralleled the street outside. Five rooms overlooked the street. The one at the far left had FAITH painted over the door, and as he walked by Dylan noticed ROSIE on the center room and SHARON on the one next to FAITH.

Dylan unlocked the door. Inside, he lit the lamp with a lucifer from a box on the stand. The yellow light from the lamp turned the pink wallpaper deep orange and the red roses were nearly black. Tired to the bone, Dylan locked the door and threw the saddle-bags over a chair. Sitting on the edge of Faith's bed, he took off his gunbelt and shucked his boots. The bed sagged in the middle. He wondered what antics had gone on there.

Twisting around, he stretched out full length on the bed. In moments, he slept, and Jared Carter stalked across his dreams.

The rumble of wagons across the Claro Bridge shook Dylan awake. He got up and pulled the curtain aside, peering through the grime collected on the glass. Mott's freight train crossed the bridge. The lead wagon came abreast of Bartley's. Its three yokes of oxen plodded stoically forward. The five-ton wagons creaked and complained as their wide eight-inch wheels raised a column of dust that increased with each passing wagon. Shouts of the bullwhackers, punctuated by cracks of bullwhips, drifted up to Dylan's window. He let the curtain drop.

The wagons were still plodding by as Dylan ate his breakfast of flapjacks and molasses. Bartley looked almost happy.

' 'Magine Mott'll round 'em up on the flat,' he said. 'They'll be a full house tonight. Maybe the only one this year.' The saloon owner turned pensive. 'You might as well stick around for the fun, Mr Dylan.'

Dylan shook his head. 'Gotta get on to Longhorn,' he said. 'A man there needs killing.'

The dust from the passing wagons had barely settled when Dylan rode Bronc out of Grant's Crossing. Longhorn was due south along Rio Claro, half a day's fast ride away. And every step Bronc took brought Nat Dylan that much closer to Jared Carter.

CHAPTER FOUR

Alton Jackson took another look at himself in the big mirror on his bedroom wall. He'd called on her several times at Rancho Vasquez, but this was the first time she'd ever visited the Wagonwheel. She'd be here soon and he wanted to present just the right image of wealth and gentility. His slightly curly hair was parted precisely in the middle and well oiled. Waves adorned the sides of his broad forehead. A fragrance of musk surrounded him like an aura.

Although he was thirty-five, lines were only beginning to show in the corners of his eyes, but deep frown lines stood perpendicular between his light brown eyebrows, even when he smiled. Hazel eyes, pencil-thin moustache, square chin – Jackson nodded to himself. Jackson stood confident in his finery: A dark Prince Albert coat with snow-white shirt, pearl-gray cravat, crystal stickpin that looked like a diamond, and gray trousers just a shade darker than the cravat. He was ready to receive Carmen San Vicente de Vasquez y Roja, heiress to the Vasquez

Grant. She must have decided that their courtship could move on to the next step – carefully chaperoned evenings together.

'Donny,' Jackson called.

Running steps sounded and a dark-haired boy of about ten came to attention in the doorway. 'Yessir, Colonel Jackson,' he said. He stood in a brace, his eyes carefully focused on a point directly above Alton Jackson's head. Jackson smiled his approval of the boy's discipline. He'd make a fine cadet.

'Miss Carmen Vasquez will soon arrive, Donny. Please put out two cups and saucers of the best china and heat some water for tea.'

The lad saluted and raced away to do the colonel's bidding.

'Buggy coming, boss.' Frenchy Durand's voice came from the front of the house. Jackson strode out to greet the woman he thought of as his bride-to-be. And in his mind, he undressed Carmen Vasquez and marveled at the ivory of her naked buttocks and a thrill rippled through his body as he applied a slender cane to the ivory flesh and she begged for more discipline.

His eyes still held an eager brightness as he stood on the porch. Carmen Vasquez drove the buggy herself, handling the matched grays with the careless skill of long practice.

Raoul Rodriguez, the Mexicali gunman, rode a big paint stallion at the buggy's side. The horse pranced as Rodriguez held him short with the reins in his left hand. His right rested lightly on his tight black breeches, inches from the butt of a nickel-plated Colt Peacemaker.

Jackson knew Rodriguez had his men spotted and was ready to fight any or all of them. But Jackson only had eyes for Carmen Vasquez. As the buggy stopped, Jackson stepped down from the porch and offered his hand to the señorita. She ignored it and descended gracefully from the buggy on her own.

'Thank you for coming, Carmen,' Jackson said, a thin smile failing to hide his irritation.

'May we go inside? What I have to say is for you alone.'

Jackson's smile broadened. 'Of course. This way.'

Again Carmen ignored his proffered hand, ascending the steps to the porch in a flurry of skirts. Rodriguez moved his stallion to stand between the buggy and the house.

The china cups sat ready on the table so Jackson indicated a chair for Carmen. 'A cup of tea, perhaps? I have some fine Indian varieties.'

Carmen gave him a curt nod and waited, her fingers drumming on the table while Jackson went through the elaborate ritual of preparing tea.

'There. Fit for a queen such as you, my dear.' Jackson raised his cup in a salute.

'Alton Jackson. I did not come here for small talk or to drink English tea. You have come to our rancho many times, and you seem to think I would consent to marry you. I am here to rid you of that misconception. I will not marry anyone for political reasons and I will not marry you for any reason. Do I make myself clear?'

Jackson sipped at his tea and looked at her with fond eyes and a half-smile. *How good it will be to discipline her,* he thought. *And after she gets used to the discipline, she'll come to seek it.*

'Do not rush to conclusions, my dear,' he said gently. 'You may not know your own mind.'

Carmen's eyes flashed. She leaped to her feet. Her chair crashed sidelong to the floor. 'Never,' she said. 'Never. As long as my heart beats, never.'

She whirled and strode swiftly to the door. There she turned, her eyes flashing. 'Never, Alton Jackson, and that is final.'

Jackson threw back his head and laughed. 'I think you will be surprised at what you will or will not do, my dear,' he said in a gay voice to her disappearing back. With a wave of his hand, he commanded the boy to clear the china away. By the time he reached the front door, Carmen Vasquez was far away; only a cloud of dust remained.

He felt a twinge of anger at her flat refusal of his advances, even though he had every confidence she would be his in the end.

As he walked through the living room, the crash of china hitting the kitchen floor made him smile. The day would not be wasted. Now he had reason to discipline Donny.

The youngster stood stiff, with his hands pressed to his legs. He stared at the shattered cup, then looked up with frightened eyes when Jackson reached the door.

'You're expected to wash and dry the china, Donny, not shatter it.'

Speechless, the boy nodded.

'Wait for me at the woodpile, young man.' Jackson stepped into his bedroom to get the braided leather quirt he used to discipline the boys.

Nat Dylan rode down Main Street with the sun to his right. He reined Bronc past the Gay Paree theater and onto River Street. He pulled his hat low to keep the sun from his eyes and loosened the Remington in its holster. Who could tell when or where he might meet Jared Carter here in Longhorn. The Monarch saloon stood on the corner of River and Taylor. Across Taylor Street, the Angus rivaled the Monarch for customers. Next door was the Iron Skillet, which sat cheek by jowl with the Hughes Hotel on the corner of River and Lincoln. The Great Western and Pacific Railway station stood across River Street from the hotel.

Dylan continued on past Solomon's Mercantile and several shingles advertising lawyers and such. He'd ridden by the courthouse on his way down Main Street, so he knew where the law was located. Now he had to find Mine Road, because that was where Marshal Rencher in Horsehead had said the Wagonwheel was. 'Ain't yet rightly a ranch,' Rencher said. 'Colonel Jackson came in with a crew, I heard, and said a herd of thirty thousand cows was coming after. Didn't say what range he planned to use. Could be tough, unless he buys land from the GW&PR.

Government gave the railroad a lot of land for building the line through here. Anyway, you'll find the Wagonwheel place on Mine Road, out past Chinatown. Mighty fancy street names for a little town, but with the railroad, I reckon Longhorn's gonna grow. You plan on working for the Wagonwheel?'

'I talked to the colonel about it,' Dylan said. 'But it may not work out.'

The streets in Longhorn were wide, but only Main and River were gravelled. Bronc's spring returned to his stride when Dylan guided him onto the rutted surface of Mine Road. Just as Marshal Rencher said, a big white house stood back from Mine Road just before it dipped down to cross a wide wash. Had to be the Wagonwheel. Dylan reined Bronc into the lane leading to the big house. A tall heavily built man stood by the porch when Dylan rode up. 'Howdy,' Dylan said. 'I'm Nat Dylan. Come to see to Colonel Jackson about a job we talked of in Horsehead a couple of days ago.'

'You're Dylan, then. I'm Frenchy Durand. The boss is around back. Tie your horse and go on around.'

Dylan dismounted and wrapped Bronc's reins around the hitching rail. 'Thanks, Frenchy. All right if I call you Frenchy?'

'Everybody else does.'

Dylan waved a hand at Durand and walked around toward the back of the house. As he turned the corner, he heard the flat splat of leather smacking

37

flesh, and the whimper of a child.

'Quiet, Donny,' Jackson said. His voice sounded almost gay. 'Take your discipline like a man.'

Dylan heard another splat, but this time the boy was silent. A third splat. The sound of quick breathing, like someone trying not to cry.

'Now, Donny. When I ask you to do the dishes, I wish you to take due care and finish the job without breaking any china, is that clear?' As Jackson spoke, Dylan watched him fingering his quirt as if he were about to hit the boy who bent over the woodpile again.

'Colonel Jackson,' Dylan said.

Jackson started. He turned to see who had spoken. Then put on a smile that was nearly a smirk. 'One moment, Mr Dylan,' Jackson said, and redirected his attention to the boy. 'Donny, I'm sure you learned your lesson. No more broken china. Is that clear?'

The boy nodded.

Viciously, Jackson brought the quirt down again.

'What do you say, Bobby?'

'Yessir, Colonel Jackson. Thank you, sir. I learned my lesson, sir. I will not break any more china, sir.' The boy's voice cracked, but he was able to speak the required litany.

'Good. Pull up your trousers and get back to your duties.'

'Yessir.' The boy gingerly hiked up his britches, pulled the suspenders over his shoulders, and sprinted for the house.

'You were saying, Mr Dylan?'

Dylan couldn't keep the distaste from his face, but what he had to do was more important. 'It's Jared Carter, Colonel,' Dylan said. 'He shot down my brothers. I'm on a killing trail; I'm after him.'

'Capital,' Jackson said. 'Come into the house. We'll talk particulars.'

Dylan grunted.

Frenchy Durand entered the house with Dylan and Jackson. He stood in the door while Jackson made his offer.

'A hundred a month and you eat here with the rest of the Wagonwheel hands,' Jackson said.

Dylan nodded. 'What about expenses?'

'Expenses?'

'I use a lot of cartridges practicing.'

'I'll pay for them. Just put them on my account at Solomon's.'

'All right. Where's Carter?' Dylan asked.

'He usually stays at the Hughes Hotel, and he leaves his buckskin at the livery stable. He drinks at the Angus or the Monarch. He also drinks at a grubby cantina in Mud Flats over across Rio Claro. I suggest you spend some time at the Monarch. He'll show.'

Jackson turned to Durand. 'Frenchy, you get Dick Rogers and Ray Stanley to accompany Dylan in case he needs help.'

'Will do, boss.'

Dylan and the two Wagonwheel men were in the Monarch when a man in gray rode by on a long-legged buckskin.

'That's Jared Carter,' Rogers said. 'Looks like he's going to the Hughes Hotel.'

Rogers loitered across River Street as Carter entered the hotel. He was still there, leaning against a post and whittling on a stick, when Carter came out and went to the Iron Skillet next door. The sun set and the streets grew dark as Carter ate. Rogers watched him put away a steak that almost covered the entire plate, a pile of mashed potatoes smothered in gravy, a large piece of pie, and three big mugs of coffee. Rogers's own stomach began to growl, but he stayed on lookout until Carter left the restaurant, stopped to pick his teeth, then walked east on River Street toward the small clapboard building that housed the *Exponent*. When he saw that Carter had settled down to read newspapers in the light of a coal-oil lamp, Rogers returned to the Monarch.

'Carter's at the *Exponent*,' Rogers said. 'Looks like he may be a while. He's reading through a pile of old papers.'

Dylan swept the Remington from his hip.

'Hey. Don't go pulling guns in here,' the bartender hollered.

'All right,' Dylan said. He thrust a sixth bullet into the cylinder and returned the Remington to its holster. 'I'll go keep watch,' he said. He put a dollar on the table. 'Have a drink and then come on out.'

Now he could execute his brothers' killer. He stood silently on the boardwalk across from the office of the *Exponent*. He could see Jared Carter examining old papers beneath a lantern. He licked his lips and waited.

Carter stood and replaced a paper. He turned the lantern down low and stopped for a moment in the doorway on the way out. Dylan was dressed in black and dark gray except for his off-white shirt. He blended into the shadow, but didn't care if Carter saw him.

Instead of walking out into the street, Carter stepped sideways into the shadows of the roof's overhang.

'Jared Carter,' Dylan shouted. 'This is Nat Dylan! It's time you paid for my brothers!' He'd given warning enough; he drew his Remington and shot Jared Carter.

Carter threw his arms wide and stumbled into the alley between the *Exponent*'s building and the one next to it. Dylan stepped carefully down the street. Wounded men and animals were dangerous. Even a dying man could pull a trigger and his bullet would kill a man just as dead as any other. Dylan catfooted to the corner of the *Exponent* building. He took off his hat and knelt at the edge of the boardwalk. At slightly lower than waist height, he peered around the corner with his right eye. Darkness kept him from seeing well, but he could tell there was nobody there. Gone.

'Rogers! Stanley! He's crawled away somewhere. Can't be far. He's hit. Get around back. Get that man!' Dylan barged into the *Exponent* and grabbed the lantern. 'Borrowing your light,' he yelled. He turned up the wick and Rogers came into the alley from the back.

'No sign of him, Dylan. You sure you hit him?'

'He fell.' Dylan held the lantern up. Dark splotches marked the boardwalk and splattered in the dust. 'He'll be under the building. Watch the other side.'

Dylan and the Wagonwheel men watched and waited, but Carter got away. They searched as well as they could with the lantern but came away empty. Eventually, Dylan called it off. 'When it gets light,' he said, 'we'll track him down.'

CHAPTER FIVE

In the morning light Dylan took the Wagonwheel men with him to town. They found Carter's blood sign two houses away from where Dylan shot him and followed him to a wagon track that ran south across the Longhorn bridge, along the side of Mud Flats, out onto the juniper flats. The spots of blood showed Carter walking south, but they suddenly disappeared.

'Someone's picked him up,' Dylan said. 'No telling where they are or where they're hiding him. Rogers, you come with me and let Stanley go back to the Wagonwheel to tell the colonel what's going on.'

Dylan led Rogers north along the wagon trail. When they topped out in a cut, gramma-grass flats spread out before them, dotted with one-seed and Utah juniper. The wagon track wound across the landscape and disappeared behind a knoll in the distance.

'All we can do is follow the road,' Dylan said. 'If we come across sign of anyone leaving it, we'll tail them.'

The sun reached its meridian before the riders reached the knoll. On the far side of the hill, sheep showed as white dots on the flat and a sheep camp sat next to a half-dry tank not more than a mile away.

'Mexicans,' Rogers said. 'Carter's thick with Mexes.'

'We'll check them out,' Dylan said. He flipped the hold-down thong off the hammer of his Remington.

Closer, Dylan saw that the sheep camp sat next to the ruins of an old adobe house. The roof was long gone and a packrat had piled a nest up against one broken-down wall. A cook fire burned between the shepherd's wagon and the old adobe. A Mexican sheepherder rustled about in the back of the wagon.

Dylan walked his horse past the adobe wall. 'We're looking for a wounded man,' he said to the sheepherder. 'He's six feet tall or so, with black hair and brown eyes. They say he's got Injun blood. He'd be wearing a gray shirt and Levis and maybe a black vest. He's wounded, and may be dead. What about it, sheepherder? Seen him?'

'*Perdon, señor. Zee Inglés.* I am not so good. *Perdon.* Perhaps maybe, *el señor,* he speaks more slowly, no?'

Dylan snorted. 'I'm not a killer, sheepherder, but you're trying my patience. Now. Have you seen a man on the wagon track? Or anything else?'

'*En el camino, señor?* The road, as you say? No . . . but *momento. . . .*'

Dylan figured the Mexican was dissembling. He sat his horse and waited.

Bronc stamped and blew. Roger's bay answered

from beyond the wagon.

'Mebbe we'd better have a look in the wagon, Dylan,' Rogers said.

'You do it,' Dylan barked. He was strung tight.

'Hey, greaser.' Rogers's saddle creaked as he dismounted. The sheepherder went to the far side of the wagon.

'Open it up, Mex,' Rogers said.

'*Sí, señor.*' The tailgate dropped, rattling on its chains. Rogers climbed inside. Something metal struck something wood. Rattles came from the wagon. 'There ain't nothing in here, Dylan,' he said. He clambered down from the wagon. 'I'll take care of the Mex.'

Dylan heard the splat of steel striking flesh and a body dropping to the ground.

'You'd better not've killed him,' Dylan said. 'He may be just a Mexican, but we ain't killers. It's the killer we're looking for. Jared Carter killed my brothers, and if he's not dead already, I'll kill him . . . or he'll kill me. Let's go on down the wagon track.'

'We go far enough, we'll hit Wilmington, Dylan. Carter's crawled off somewhere to die. We're not gonna find him.'

'I got a feeling Jared Carter's not dead. He walked to the road. He could have walked away from it. If we don't find him, maybe he'll find us.' Dylan reined Bronc away from the old adobe. 'We'll follow the road till sundown. If we don't find Carter, we'll go back to Longhorn and wait. He'll show his face before long.'

As he turned Bronc, Dylan caught a rustling sound that seemed to come from beneath the rat nest. He motioned Rogers to be quiet and walked Bronc toward the road.

A few moments later, dry sticks crackled and Jared Carter dragged himself from beneath the packrat nest. His breath came in great gasps and sometimes he'd moan deep in his chest. He crawled to the wagon and used the wheel to pull himself upright. Strips of off-white cloth bound pads to his side and back. Blood tinged them. Carter shook his head like he was trying to get rid of a dizzy spell. He took a deep breath. Holding on to the wagon, he shuffled sideways around to where the sheepherder lay. He stopped at the far rear wheel. Dylan noticed Carter was barefoot. Where were his boots? Why didn't Rogers find them in the wagon?

The Mexican lay curled in a foetal ball, his arms covering his head. His chest moved. He was alive. His straw hat, knocked flying by Rogers's pistol barrel, lay on the ground. Carter took another deep breath. Standing up seemed to help him gain strength. His whole attention was on the Mexican. He didn't notice Dylan and Rogers walking their horses closer.

Carter took two steps away from the wagon and went to his knees beside the fallen sheepherder. He put a hand on the man's shoulder. Dylan swept his Remington from its holster, cocking the hammer as he drew. Carter froze at the sound.

'Well, well, Jared Carter,' Nat Dylan said. 'I see you're not dead after all.'

Carter ignored Dylan and grunted as he rolled the sheepherder face up. The Mexican's eyelids fluttered.

'Rami? *Amigo?*'

The sheepherder groaned.

'Dylan, what're you waiting on? That's the man what killed your brothers!' Rogers eared back the hammer of his six-gun.

Carter didn't even turn his head. He just reached out a hand to the sheepherder's brow. The Mexican's eyelids fluttered again.

'Rami!' Carter said. He shook the man's shoulder.

'Oooh, Señor Carter. I feel broken apart. Do I lie in pieces?'

Dylan spoke. 'That's enough, Carter. I'd say it's time we had it out.'

Carter knelt there, barefoot, shirt in tatters, torso wrapped with cloth strips, no hat, no gun.

'All right, Dylan,' he said, his voice low and the words short and hard. 'Take a good look. Do you see a gun? I can hardly stand, much less pull iron.

'Back then, they called me the Carter Kid, because that's what I was. I acted like a kid and I had my pride.

'I rode into Ouray and your giant of a brother tried to run me out of town. I hit him like your rider hit the Mexican. I didn't want to fight your brothers, Dylan, I wanted sleep. I'd been in the saddle more days than I wanted to count. Your brothers came gunning for me, Dylan, just because I knocked one of them down.

47

'I don't know who shot first, but when it ended, your brothers were dead and I was wounded. I barely made it to Mobeetie.

'I'm here, and you've shot a hole in me. You want to finish it up, you'd better shoot now. Then you'll want to kill Rami and your rider, too, because they'll know you shot an unarmed man.'

Carter stopped talking. After a moment, he struggled to his feet, got some water, and knelt again to give it to the sheepherder he called Rami.

Dylan released the hammer of his Remington and slid it back into its holster.

'What in hell are you doing, Dylan?' Rogers asked.

'Like he says, Rogers. Look at him. Wounded. Unarmed. Weak. Killing him would be murder. I'm not a killer.

'Carter, you'll live. You stay here. When you're healed, we'll meet again and I'll kill you, or you me. Come on, Rogers.'

Dylan wheeled Bronc and walked him back up the wagon road toward Longhorn. Rogers holstered his six-gun and followed.

For all his polite words and gentlemanly manners, Alton Jackson was angry. Nat Dylan could read the heightened color in the rancher's cheeks, the brightness in his eyes, and the growing band of red, blood-infused tissue above his tight collar. The signs said anger, but Jackson's words were soft and low. 'You're telling me, Mr Dylan, that Jared Carter is badly wounded. You saw him? You talked to him?

48

And you left him alive?'

'I did.'

'And I thought you were a man who didn't need direct orders to get a job done.' The venom in Jackson's softly spoken words made Dylan wonder if maybe he'd die of rat-poisoning. Jackson continued, 'I think you should take a rest, Mr Dylan. Spend a few days in town. Have a drink or two. Play some poker. I understand you're adept at games of chance. Frenchy can finish your job with Jared Carter. That man has been nosing around Wagonwheel business, and I will not have it.'

'Jared Carter won't kill easy,' Dylan said.

'From what you said, he's badly wounded and unable to move. Now's the time to strike,' Jackson retorted.

'I want him, Mr Jackson, don't you misunderstand. But it ain't right to shoot a man who can't defend himself. I won't be known as a cheater or a killer, and killing a helpless unarmed man is cheating in my book.'

Jackson put on his thin-lipped rattlesnake smile. 'Don't you worry yourself about the moral implications of the situation,' he said, using silver-dollar words. 'You rest yourself. You've done more than your share by getting lead into Jared Carter. Just relax and let the Wagonwheel boys take care of the rest.'

'I'm telling you, Colonel. Jared Carter's a curly wolf from the high timber. He won't be there when your boys go hunting, and he won't show up until he's good and ready. And then him and me will have it out. It don't matter what you say or do, that's the way it'll be.'

'You may leave now, Mr Dylan,' Jackson said, pointing at the door.

Dylan left, mounting Bronc at the hitching rail, but before he could turn the horse, he heard the whack of an open hand and the yelp of a boy. Jackson was taking his frustrations out on the youngsters again. Dylan frowned.

A lad burst from the house with tears in his eyes, running toward the bunkhouse. 'Mr Durand,' he called.

Frenchy appeared in the doorway. The boy skidded to a halt and stood at attention as he delivered his message.

'Mr Durand, sir. Colonel Jackson would appreciate your company in the house, sir.'

Durand patted the boy on the head and strode toward the Wagonwheel headquarters. The youngster dogtrotted at his heels. Dylan watched the foreman enter the house and decided he'd stick around to see what happened.

Moments later, Durand slammed the screen door open and shouted. 'Rogers. Nueces. Jones. Peters.'

Answers came from different parts of the grounds. Dylan threw a leg over the saddle horn and started fiddling with the makings. No one paid him a flicker of attention.

'Get your horses,' Durand said. 'An' get grub for three days from Cookie.' His eyes shone. 'We're going hunting, so bring plenty of cartridges.'

Dylan struck a lucifer on his pants and lit the smoke that dangled from his lips. He inhaled the acrid Bull Durham and watched. After the five Wagonwheel men thundered away to the north, Dylan nudged Bronc over to the kitchen door. Cookie came to see who it was. 'I'm gonna need a bait of grub, too, Cookie,' Dylan said in his most disarming tone. The cook nodded and disappeared into the pantry. Moments later he reappeared with a bulging flour sack.

'Biscuits and bacon,' the cook said, 'and some flour and salt and a little coffee. You'll have to get your own water, frying pan, and coffee pot.'

'Oh, I can do that; done it more'n once before.' Dylan took the bag. He'd fill his canteen from the river and brew coffee in his tin cup if he had to.

The five men were easy to follow. They didn't worry about covering their trail and they didn't expect anyone to come after them. If they were successful, Jared Carter would disappear and no one would ever know what happened to him.

The sheep camp by the adobe wall was gone when the riders got there, but it took no Apache to trail a flock of sheep. The new camp was in a hollow near Carrizo Creek. Several gnarled cottonwoods stood on the creek banks. The rim of the hollow was covered with juniper and scrub oak, giving Dylan ample cover from which to watch.

No one was in camp when the Wagonwheel men arrived. 'We'll wait. The herder'll come back before

51

dark.' Dylan heard Durand's voice plainly. He settled down in a copse of juniper to see what happened when Ramirez the sheepherder came back.

He dozed in the hot afternoon sun, then came awake at a shout from one of the riders.

'There he is!'

Seeing horses in camp, Ramirez turned to run, but the Wagonwheel riders were too quick. The Texan Nueces was on his horse in a flying leap and shaking out a loop in his lariat as the Mexican dodged through the high grass. Seconds later, his loop dropped over Rami's head and the rider dragged the hapless Mexican back to camp.

'There's a boy out there, too, Frenchy,' Nueces said when he got back to the fire.

'Get 'im.'

Nueces left to chase the boy down.

Frenchy Durand tied Ramirez to a wagon wheel. Then he slapped him in the face with his open, horny hand. The sheepherder's head snapped around and a trickle of blood started at the corner of his mouth.

'Jared Carter was in your camp two days ago, Mex. Where is he?'

Ramirez shook his head and let loose a torrent of Spanish, obviously imploring for mercy and denying anything to do with Carter and begging with teary eyes and slobbery mouth.

Dick Rogers walked up to Ramirez and shoved the muzzle of his Colt into the soft flesh beneath the Mexican's jaw. 'Remember me, Mex? I'm the one that like to broke your noggin with this gun. Now don't tell me you don't know where Jared Carter's at.'

The Mexican stopped babbling, but kept shaking his head.

Frenchy Durand got a running iron from his saddle and shoved it in the fire. Ramirez watched askance, the whites of his eyes showing like a frightened colt's.

Nueces rode up with the kicking, screaming boy.

'Tie him to the cottonwood,' Durand ordered. Nueces complied. Then Durand picked the running iron out of the fire with a gloved hand. Grabbing the boy by the jaw, Durand twisted his face and placed the iron next to his right eye. He looked at Ramirez, who watched with horror in his eyes.

'Now, Mex. Tell me. Where's Jared Carter?'

'Oh, no, *señor*. He is only a child. *Por favor.*'

'Nits grow into lice,' Durand said, a sneer on his face. He moved the iron closer. The boy strained to get away.

'No, no, no, *Madre de Dios*. No. I will tell you, *señor*. Jared Carter is in a cave on the side of the hill you call Mill Valley Knoll.'

'That's better,' Durand said with a smile and plunged the hot iron through the boy's eye and into his brain. The boy went limp. Dylan felt the bile rise in his throat.

Durand withdrew the sputtering iron and dropped it on the ground. Ramirez hung from his bonds, head down, weeping. Durand drew his six-gun and shot the sheepherder.

'Done,' he said. 'Now let's ride for Mill Valley Knoll.' The Wagonwheel men thundered away to the south-west.

Nat Dylan rode Bronc to the sheep camp. Both man and boy were dead. Dylan found a shovel in the wagon. At least he could dig them shallow graves.

CHAPTER SIX

Once he'd thought about it, Nat Dylan saw that burying the two sheepherders on the spot was not the right thing to do. He wrapped the bodies in blankets, holding his breath against the stench of burnt flesh and death-loosened bowels, and put them in the sheep-camp wagon. The team was picketed near the tank, so Dylan harnessed the horses and hitched them to the wagon traces. He tied Bronc to the tailgate and started for Longhorn.

Two hours later, he pulled the team to a stop in front of Sheriff Campbell's office at the county courthouse building.

'Howdy, Dylan,' the sheriff said from the door. 'Something on your mind?'

'I found two dead sheepmen out south of here. Thought you'd want a look at them.'

'Sheepherders? Let me see.'

Dylan thumbed over his shoulder at the bodies. 'Help yourself.'

Sheriff Campbell said nothing as he examined the

bodies, though he lingered over the boy.

'Found 'em, did you?'

'They were dead when I got there.'

Campbell raised an eyebrow at Dylan's choice of words. 'That boy died hard, Dylan. You wouldn't know anything about that now, would you?'

'I said they were dead when I got there.'

'Yeah. I heard you. And you didn't see anything, either. Right?'

Dylan didn't answer. He wouldn't lie, but he couldn't tattle on the brand he rode for, either. Still, the callous way Frenchy Durand had killed the Mexicans went against Dylan's sense of fairness.

'Thought I'd take the bodies home, wherever that is,' Dylan said, eventually. 'Thought maybe you could tell me where to go.'

'Go back across the bridge and take the wagon road west through Mud Flats to Fool's Hollow. You'll find a track on the far side that leads south. You'll want to go to Rancho Vasquez and see Don Orlando.'

Dylan waited.

'Whereabouts did you find the bodies?'

Dylan told him.

'What about the sheep?'

'Looked like the dogs was watching them.'

The sheriff nodded. 'All right. Take them away.'

Dylan clucked at the team and maneuvered the wagon around to head back toward Rio Claro. Bronc came along behind. As the wagon rumbled over the bridge, Dylan saw a cloud of dust coming toward town. In moments, he recognized Alton Jackson, driving a light buggy. Jackson must have recognized Dylan, too, because he slowed the buggy and stopped. Dylan reined the shepherd's horses to a halt.

'Thought you were playing cards,' Jackson said. 'Whose wagon?'

'Dead man's.'

'And why might you be driving a dead man's wagon?'

'Taking him home.'

'Since when are you the angel of mercy, Dylan?'

'Two men lie dead in this wagon, Colonel Jackson. Mercy has nothing to do with it. Just decency.'

Jackson laughed. 'You? Decent?'

Dylan's eyes took on the color of cold steel and his voice a sharp cutting edge. 'Alton Jackson,' he said, 'I watched your foreman kill these two with no reason, and one of them just a young boy. Now you're paying my wages, so I said nothing to Sheriff Campbell, but the whole thing wasn't right; it ain't right. I can't bring them back to life. The least I can do is see that they get home so their folks can bury them proper. Now leave me go.'

Jackson sneered. 'What're you worried about two Mex sheepherders for? One or two more or less doesn't mean a hell of a lot in my book. What's got you so upset?'

'They died for no good reason.'

'Being Mex isn't reason enough?'

Dylan stared at the nattily dressed rancher. He could even smell the rose water the man used so liberally. Had he no sense of honor? A ripple of distaste rolled through Dylan's mind. Still, he'd been paid for the month and his honor said he must ride for the brand. He swallowed his anger.

'If it's just the same with you, sir. I'll be moving on. Can't hurt to take these dead men home.'

'Whatever. But report to me when you return. I think there are things we must clarify.'

'Yes, sir. I'll do that. Now, I'll be going.' Dylan slapped the reins on the team's backs and the sheep-camp wagon with its load of grief rattled down the track toward Fool's Hollow.

The miles dropped slowly behind the lumbering wagon, giving Dylan time to reflect on what had happened since he came to Longhorn. It was not as easy to exact revenge as he'd thought. Five years ago at fifteen, he'd burned with hate for the man who'd killed his brothers. Now he was finding out what kind of man Jared Carter was and that killing him was not a simple thing to do. His older brothers had made a pet of Dylan after his mother died. They'd gone out of their way to make sure he went to school and all. But even as a youngster, he realized that folks in town didn't like his brothers. Perhaps they'd been respected and feared for their strong arms and quick guns, but none followed the Dylans because of their honor or their good deeds.

Miss Shoemeister, the schoolmarm who was Nat Dylan's first love, spoke often of an ancient king of England. 'His name was Arthur,' she'd said. 'He created a round table for his knights, round so there was no head nor foot and each knight would be seated equal to all the others. King Arthur urged his knights to battle evil and succor the weak. It was their creed that mere might did not make right.'

A light always came to Miss Shoemeister's eyes when she spoke of King Arthur. Perhaps she wished she'd lived way back then. Because of her, Nat Dylan promised himself always to be polite to womenfolk and not take advantage of the weak. That's what a strong man was supposed to do, he felt.

Now he drove toward Rancho Vasquez with the sheepherder Ramirez and the boy Juan dead in the bed of the wagon. They didn't have to die. Durand got his information. He had no call to kill them. Tears of frustration welled in Nat Dylan's eyes. He swiped them away with an impatient fist and concentrated on delivering his sad load.

The sheep-camp wagon rattled up to the main gate at Rancho Vasquez in the dark of a moonless night.

'*Alto. Quien es?*' A guard challenged Dylan.

'The name's Nat Dylan. I want to talk to Don Orlando Vasquez.'

'*Uno momento,*' said the guard. A horse galloped away toward the hacienda. Moments later, three horses – no, four – came thundering toward the gate. They slid to a halt, sending a cloud of dust over the wagon.

'I am Orlando Vasquez,' said a voice from among the riders.

'Two of your sheepherders got killed down near

Toele. I brung them home.'

A gasp escaped one rider. 'I am Carmen Vasquez,' a woman's voice said. 'Are they Ramirez and Juan?'

'Yes, ma'am.'

'And you, Señor Dylan. Are you not the killer who shot Jared Carter?'

'Yes, ma'am. I shot him, but I ain't no killer, or he'd be dead. We just got an old score to settle. That's all.'

'And you did not kill poor Ramirez and the boy Juan?'

'No, ma'am. But I seen it, and it wasn't pretty. Before they died, they told five men where Jared Carter is hiding.'

'They told of *Pueblo Fantasma*, the village of ghosts?'

'No, ma'am. Ramirez said Carter is holed up in a cave at Mill Valley Knoll.'

'He's at Mill Valley Knoll?'

'That's what Ramirez said, ma'am, and I don't think he was in a position to lie.'

A rider pounded away and returned with a torch held high. Its light showed a white-haired patriarch dressed in loose white shirt and dark trousers. The woman rode astride, in a split riding skirt. Her beautiful face was drawn up in anguish. Dylan's heart thumped. He'd not seen such a fine woman since Miss Rebecca Shoemeister. The third rider was a big Mexican in short jacket and tight trousers with silver conchos down the sides. Twin pearl-handled revolvers rode high on his hips and the torchlight

60

glinted on twin rows of bullets on his gunbelt.

At the slight motion of the patriarch's hand, the guard stepped out and opened the gate. The four came through, torch held high.

'Where are my men?'

Dylan jerked a thumb at the blanket-shrouded corpses.

'Ramon. Drive the wagon to the hacienda, *por favor*. And have two men ride to the sheep camp, *immediamente*,' the Don ordered.

'*Sí, Patron*,' the man with the torch answered. He dismounted. '*Con permiso*,' he said to Dylan, holding his hand out for the reins.

Dylan surrendered them and went back to untie Bronc. He mounted and turned to the Vasquez riders.

'I'll be getting back to Longhorn,' he said.

Carmen Vasquez spoke. 'Thank you, Señor Dylan. You are a man of honor. We will put them to rest.'

Her rich contralto voice thrilled Dylan, but there was nothing to do but rein Bronc around and leave the way he had come.

A wagon rattled up to Wagonwheel headquarters with three men in the bed: one dead, one half dead, and one wounded. A Mormon farmer drove the rig, and Doc Richards came along behind in his one-horse buggy. Nat Dylan watched from the bunkhouse door.

'Jared Carter asked us to see about these men at Mill Valley Knoll,' the Mormon said to Alton Jackson.

'Asked us to get Doc Richards. Carter said they was your men, but he'd promised to send help; said he wouldn't have good men die because they rode for the wrong brand.'

Jackson sputtered.

'Colonel Jackson, may we take these men inside? I must deprive one young man of his leg, but not his life – if we're lucky,' the doctor said.

'Dylan. Lend a hand,' Jackson ordered. Nat Dylan helped, not so much because Jackson ordered him as because he was curious about what had happened at Mill Valley Knoll.

Rogers and Durand had come in the day before, giving the idea, without actually saying so, that Jared Carter had killed the other three and that a big Mexican shootist had come to his aid. That, said Durand, is why they'd failed to get Carter. Dylan smiled to himself. Jared Carter was not an easy man to kill. He had friends.

Dylan and the Mormon, who said his name was Wilford Snow, carried the two wounded men into the house on litters made of blankets and poles.

'Put him on the kitchen table,' Doc Richards ordered, pointing to the rider with the wounded leg.

'Boil me some water,' he said to the cook. 'And I'll need some clean cloth for bandages.'

'His name's Dan Jones,' Dylan said.

'Regardless of his name, I must take his leg,' the doctor said. 'He cut the flow of blood with a tourniquet and the flesh has gone dead, but the tourniquet did save his life.'

The doctor turned to Dylan. 'I'm going to chloroform this man. He's dehydrated and he's lost blood, but perhaps I can save him. Will you help?'

Dylan nodded. 'Just tell me what to do.'

The doctor positioned the chloroform mask over Jones's mouth and nose. 'I'll need you to drip chloroform on the gauze of the mask a drop at a time. You must have a steady hand, and this operation won't be pleasant.'

'I'll be fine.'

'Good. Now. Uncork the bottle and administer three drops of chloroform, if you please.' Doc Richards turned to the Mormon. 'Please go take care of that poor dead chap, if you would, Brother Snow. This shouldn't take an hour. I'd be pleased if you'd wait outside until I'm finished.'

Fetching a scalpel and a bone saw from his medical bag, the doctor went to work, with Dylan watching his every move. He worked swiftly, and Jones's leg was off and the stump cauterized, sutured, and bandaged in just over half an hour.

'Get rid of that leg,' Dr Richards ordered the cook. 'He'll not want to see it again.

'He may go into shock when he finds out his leg is gone, but I have no alternative but to put him in the bunkhouse. For the moment, however, we can leave him here while I suture the flesh wound in the other cowboy's *gluteus maximus*.'

'*Gluteus maximus?*' Dylan said.

'Butt, to most people.'

'Oh.' Dylan felt foolish but followed the doctor

63

into the living room.

Jackson glared and Peters remained silent except for a yelp or two as Doc Richards sewed the lips of the flesh wound together.

'You'll not be sitting on that for a week or so, young man. You can remove the stitches in about ten days' time, just to be sure.'

'How much do we owe you, Doctor?' Jackson's voice trembled with suppressed anger.

'To me, you owe ten dollars, including the house call and the operation. To Jared Carter, you owe the lives of these men, if young Jones makes it.'

Jackson did not meet the doctor's eyes as he dug an eagle from his pocket and handed it to him.

Dylan followed the doctor outside.

'Could you help me with this man?' Wilford Snow asked. Dylan nodded and helped him carry the bloating, stinking body of Nueces the Texan to the barn.

'Not a job I'd want to do every day,' Snow said as they turned the body onto the straw in an empty stall.

'But you did it. How come you went all the way to Mill Valley Knoll?' Dylan asked.

'Me and my boy was about a mile from Sunrise – that's the Mormon settlement south-west of Longhorn – when we met two riders, a Mexican on a big paint and a dark hatless man I first took for a red man. He said he was Jared Carter, brother to Jason Carter of the JC Ranch on Bent Creek, and asked if we might do him a favor.

'Now, our folks know Jason Carter right well, and

64

he's always been a good neighbor. So I told Jared I would gladly do him a favor. He said he reckoned there were two wounded men at Mill Valley Knoll and maybe one dead body. He wanted to know if I'd go see about them, as he'd promised one of them that he'd get help.

' "I told that man I wouldn't let him die," ' Jared said, and he looked to me for help.

'Well, I sent that boy of mine – he's going on ten – for Doc Richards and I lined out for Mill Valley Knoll. Lucky we got there when we did, or those men woulda died of thirst. I reckon Jared Carter kept his promise, and I'm happy to have helped.'

Dylan pursed his lips. He remembered how Dick Rogers had come in on a wind-broken horse, wild-eyed and calling for more men. But before they could get their equipment together and leave, Frenchy Durand had ridden in and said it was no use. Neither man had said a word about Jones and Peters lying wounded at Mill Valley Knoll, so now Dylan knew they had just given up on them and left them to die.

'Damn!' Dylan swore. Snow lifted an eyebrow.

'Some people just ain't got a single grain of human kindness,' Dylan growled. 'They're only happy when someone else's blood is on the ground.'

Obviously, Snow had no idea what Dylan was talking about. 'Well,' he said, 'this country needs the likes of Jason and Jared Carter, I'd say. They and I ain't of the same faith, but they're men I could trust with my life . . . would, if it came to that.'

Dylan stared at the ground and scuffed at a clod with his boot toe. He'd come to Longhorn to settle an old score, yet found himself respecting the target of his revenge.

CHAPTER SEVEN

Alton Jackson raced his buggy into the yard of the Double Diamond headquarters, raising billowing dust that could be seen from the Blue Mountains, if the Apaches were watching. Nat Dylan followed at a respectable distance, his roan cantering along the windward side of the road, out of Jackson's dust. Jackson had sent Durand and half a dozen riders off on some errand, so Dylan was the only man left to ride shotgun for him.

Jed Baker met Jackson, ready to care for the matched team of chestnut fillies. 'Morning, Colonel,' the cowboy said, but the expression on his face did not reflect the courtesy of his greeting.

Here's a man who sees right through Colonel Alton Jackson, Dylan thought.

'I won't be here long, Baker. Give the horses a drink, but don't unharness them.' Jackson descended from the buggy and handed Baker the reins. He strode into the ranch house without even knocking, as if he already owned the spread.

'You might as well step down,' Baker said to Dylan. 'I'll water your pony for you.'

'I'll come along with you,' Dylan said as he swung down.

Baker unhitched the team and clipped the traces to the rings on their harnesses. 'Wonder why he uses a team with that light buggy?' Baker said. 'Most folks would pull it with one horse.'

'Colonel Jackson's a man in a hurry. He likes to move at a run and he'll use that buggy whip right quick if the ponies ain't fast enough for him,' Dylan said.

'I've seen how he's mighty impatient. And I've seen how he's quick to beat on things, be it horses or boys. Why's a kid like you riding for a man like him?'

'We're headed in somewhat the same direction,' Dylan said. 'I've been paid for a month and I still have a week and some to go.'

'You'd better look to your hole card,' Baker said. 'I don't trust that man.'

'Trust's got nothing to do with it,' said Dylan. 'He paid me up front. He's buying the ammunition for me to practice with, so he calls the shots and I ride where he tells me to . . . mostly.'

Horses watered, the two men led them to a shady spot beneath the apple trees of the Double Diamond orchard. Green fruit festooned the trees and Dylan plucked one that showed a faint tinge of red. 'Always did like green apples,' he said. He rubbed the fruit to a high shine on his shirtsleeve and took a big bite. Juice spurted from the apple and Dylan had to slurp to keep it from getting away. 'Now that's first-rate,' he said. The tart fragrance of ripening apple filled the air.

'Smells like green apple to me,' Baker said with a grin. 'Ate so many one time that I got a hell of a bellyache. That kinda threw me off green apples.'

Dylan took another bite.

'You can sit in that chair on the porch until you're ready to leave,' offered Baker. 'I got chores to do.'

Dylan nodded, walking toward the porch as he finished the apple. He threw the core at a bunch of chickens, which battled over the treat. Dylan grinned. *Just like folks*, he thought, *fighting over scraps*.

He settled in the armless chair, tipping it back to lean against the wall. Only then did he notice the voices coming from the open window.

'You said I could pay off the note after round-up, Jackson. You put it in writing, and I have that letter in my safe.'

'Things have come up, Willard. I need the cash. You'll have to round up your cows now if you want to keep your ranch. I'll give you till the tenth of August to pay off the note I hold on you.'

'That's only two weeks, Jackson. How do you expect me to get cattle together and find a buyer in that time?'

'Look, Willard. I could have demanded your money the moment I came into this country, but I've got bigger plans than taking over your two-bit outfit. As of right now, my plans require cash. Sell those cows.'

There was silence for some time, then the sound of something slapping down on a table or a desk.

'You don't have a grain of human kindness, do you, Jackson? And you couldn't care less what happens to the Double Diamond?'

'Your little outfit is of no use to me, Willard. You say you run nine thousand head of cattle; sell enough to pay me ten thousand dollars. That's all I ask.'

Milo Willard said nothing.

'You have until August tenth. No more.'

Dylan heard footsteps coming across the room, but he made no move. Jackson burst from the house and was two steps down from the porch before he noticed Dylan. 'Well. Don't sit there with your thumb in your mouth. Get moving. I'm ready to leave.'

Dylan stood up and shrugged his gun into place, watching Jackson with a baleful stare.

'All right. All right. So I didn't hire you to hitch teams. It wouldn't hurt your gunman's pride to help out a little, would it?'

Dylan said nothing. He merely brushed past Jackson on his way to the orchard for his horse. He mounted Bronc and walked him over to the buggy. He threw a leg over the saddle horn, took the makings from a vest pocket, and started building a smoke.

'Jeb Baker!' Jackson shouted.

The Double Diamond cowboy came from the barn. 'Leaving already, Colonel? I'll get those fillies hitched up.'

Jackson fidgeted all the while Baker was getting

70

the buggy ready, walking this way and that. *Doesn't look like a man who holds all the aces*, thought Dylan. *Acts like he's about to lose all he's got. Looks mighty worried to me.*

'There you go, Colonel,' Baker said, leading the team and buggy over. 'The ponies had a good drink and a few minutes on the grass in the orchard. They'll do fine.'

Jackson grunted as he clambered into the buggy. Grabbing the buggy whip, he flicked the team sharply, right and left, and sawed them into a running turn with a heavy hand on the reins. Dylan took one more drag on the Bull Durham cigarette in his fingers, then ground it out on the saddle horn.

'Didn't have to whip them fillies,' Dylan heard Baker grumble. He put his roan into an easy canter and followed the dust of Alton Jackson's buggy.

The colonel was waiting with the buggy whip in his hand when Dylan rode up to the Wagonwheel headquarters.

'Nat Dylan,' he said, accenting his words by slapping the shaft of the whip into his open palm. 'I hired you, *whack*, to kill Jared Carter, *whack*, now get the job done, *whack whack*.

Alton Jackson slapped the quirt against his booted leg again and again. The town was starting to wonder when the 30,000 head of cattle he had promised would arrive. That meddler Jared Carter was still alive. Carmen Vasquez was cold as ice toward him.

71

Only the Double Diamond deal was going according to plan.

Jackson's strongbox held little more than the fifteen hundred dollars he'd taken to settle those sodbuster migrants. He needed the ten thousand due from Milo Willard. If things didn't start falling into place, he might have to take drastic steps.

Frenchy Durand and his remaining riders were shepherding the sodbusters to a campsite on Levine Creek. Jackson's four boys hovered just out of sight. One stood at the front door. Another was near the kitchen. Sounds from upstairs said the others were cleaning the bedroom. All four moved like ghosts, fearful of Jackson's temper and discipline. He smiled as he remembered the red stripes his quirt brought to bare young bottoms. Perhaps something would happen yet today to require discipline. Saliva rushed to Jackson's mouth, forcing him to swallow. The corners of his mouth twitched. He smacked his britches with the quirt again.

Measured blasts from a pistol sounded from the wash back of the house. Dylan was practicing again. Damn. If he was such a quick gun, why didn't he just ride out and shoot Carter down? Jackson smashed the quirt against his leg. Six quick shots came from the wash.

Damn.

More shots erupted. Dylan would shoot up a whole box of shells out there, and cartridges cost money. It was part of the deal. Jackson now wished he'd not acquiesced to Dylan's demand for payment in advance, but he could do nothing about that. There was something about Dylan that kept Jackson from pushing him too hard. True, he stood no more than five-seven, a good six inches less than Jackson. He probably weighed no more than one-forty after a full meal, but his steady stare and his coiled-spring tension made Jackson wary.

The shooting stopped.

'James,' Jackson called. A youngster with mulatto features came at a trot.

'Yes, sir, Colonel Jackson,' he said, bracing to attention at Jackson's side.

'Go ask Mister Dylan to join me,' Jackson ordered. The boy ran toward the wash.

Minutes later, he returned. 'Mr Dylan said he'd be along directly, Colonel. That's what he said.' The boy's large dark eyes searched Jackson's face for signs a reprimand was coming. Jackson slapped his leg with the quirt, enjoying the boy's flinch.

'That will be all,' he said.

'Thank you, Colonel Jackson, sir,' the boy said. He backed silently to his position near the kitchen door. Once there, he seemed to fade into the woodwork, hardly breathing and standing at parade rest, his hands crossed at the small of his back.

Dylan tapped at the screen door.

'Come,' Jackson ordered.

Dylan entered, moving to a wall with no windows as if he didn't want to be silhouetted by light from outside. He stood relaxed, both hands hanging loosely at his sides, his feet spread shoulder-width apart, his knees slightly flexed. He looked ready for a gunfight.

'How was practice?' Jackson asked.

After a long moment Dylan said, 'I hit what I shoot at.'

'You don't say.' Jackson could not resist a verbal jab. 'Seems Jared Carter is still alive. Weren't you to kill him?'

'I will.'

'When?'

'When the right time comes. When it does come, we'll know it, him and me . . . he and I.'

Jackson cracked the quirt against his leg and Dylan palmed and cocked his Remington. Before he could react, Jackson was looking at the very big bore of Dylan's .45. He tried to speak, but the mouth in which saliva had so recently flowed was suddenly dry as the sandy wash out back.

'God . . . Dylan! What? Why on earth are you pointing that pistol at me?'

'I've seen how you like to beat on people, Jackson. I'm a whole lot littler than you, but I got no intention of letting you cut me with that quirt. I ain't one of your orphan boys, orphan though I am. And I'll not have you threatening me with a whipping.' Dylan held the cocked Remington steady on Jackson's midriff as he spoke.

'My God, boy. I had no such intent. You're a man grown and as such are in no need of my discipline. Now put that weapon away. We are in the house, after all.' Jackson's words tumbled over each other in his haste to reassure Dylan.

The young gunman skewered Jackson with his eyes. Without dropping his gaze, he let the Remington's hammer down and returned the pistol to the holster behind his right hip.

'Now, what did you want me for?' he asked.

Jackson licked his dry lips. 'Nothing special. Just wondering how you were making out on the subject for which you were hired.'

Dylan's cold eyes held Jackson like a snake holds a mouse with its stare. 'Mister Jackson,' he said, not using the title of 'Colonel' that Jackson preferred. 'I followed Jared Carter through the Wasatch Mountains and the badlands to Moab, and on down the Trail 'til I got here. Carter shot my three brothers. My only kin. I swore on their dead bodies to pay him back. I shot him once the other night, but his life has a charm, and it ain't right to kill a man who can't fight back. In my book, if a man can't do what's right, he's no man at all. Now, Mister Jackson. I will kill Jared Carter . . . or he'll kill me. We'll put right what's between us, but I won't murder him.'

Jackson nodded, not trusting himself to speak. Dylan sauntered out without another word.

So. Dylan was burdened with a warped sense of chivalry. Well. That meant something else had to be done. Suddenly, a smile broke out on Jackson's face. If he played his cards right, maybe he could bag two chickens in a single net.

The sound of hoofs came through the open window as Frenchy Durand and the Wagonwheel

75

riders pounded into the yard. Jackson went out on the front porch.

'How'd it go, Frenchy?'

'Without a hitch, boss. Them sodbusters is camped on Levine Creek. Ain't got much grub, though, and not a good gun among them.'

'They'll get along. Come in, Frenchy. I have something I'd like to discuss with you. In private.'

Nat Dylan knew Alton Jackson and Frenchy Durand were up to something they didn't want him to know about. Maybe his youth caused them to underestimate his intelligence. Maybe they just underestimated everyone. Only a numbskull would be unable to read the meaningful looks and knowing smirks that passed between the two men.

Dylan knew people tended to overlook him because he was small and slim and wore a blank unconcerned look on his face. The look was something he'd carefully cultivated since Jared Carter killed his brothers and he'd had to make it on his own. A blank look and youthful countenance served well at the gambling tables where Nat Dylan won more often than he lost, and when it came to gambling with a gun, Dylan lost not at all.

Dylan knew the importance of information. The more you knew about what was going on, the less likely you were to be blindsided by something you didn't expect. Jackson and Durand had not let him or anybody else in on whatever it was they were hatching up, so Dylan decided to stick close and keep his eyes and ears open, along with his nose and his mind.

Jackson held a $10,000 note over Milo Willard's head and Dylan had heard Frenchy Durand say something about sodbusters camped on Levine Creek, which was on Double Diamond land. Jackson and Durand were plotting, and Dylan wanted to find out what.

Dylan had just saddled Bronc to ride into Longhorn when Frenchy and Ray Stanley came to the corral for four mounts and the fillies that pulled Jackson's buggy. So Dylan followed naturally when they rode back to the house. He didn't say a word, just acted like he was supposed to go along.

Jackson gave him a sharp look as he climbed into the buggy, but said nothing. When Jackson pulled out, Durand and Stanley took outrider positions and Monty Wells and Gib Brewster backed them. Dylan followed as if he were to go along.

The group followed the wagon road toward the Double Diamond, raising enough dust for a troop of cavalry. The sun came down hot and made the horses sweat. Dust soon caked their hides. Several miles north of the Double Diamond, Durand signaled, and the cavalcade turned east, following a whisper of a trail. Had there not been fairly fresh wagon tracks there, it would have been difficult to identify the trail at all.

Jackson slowed his team to a brisk walk. Durand and Stanley rode out front, showing the others the trail. Dylan came on behind and to the south, out of the dust.

Dylan surveyed the range. Though he was no

77

cowman, he could see tall gramma grass and chamise in full leaf. This part of the Double Diamond had not been grazed down. There was plenty of feed, even to Dylan's eyes.

The land lay quite flat up to a low line of hills that bordered Rio Claro. Juniper and the occasional stand of scrub oak dotted the landscape, but there was not a cow in sight. Dylan wondered if Willard would be able to gather cattle enough to pay his debt. Then again, maybe Jackson was banking on Willard being unable to redeem the note.

Greenery showed to the south. A stream, most likely, Dylan thought. Soon the wagon tracks paralleled the water, still moving east. Now Dylan knew they were riding for the camp of sodbusters Durand had talked about.

The group topped out above the camp in a great plume of dust. The camp looked strange, even to Dylan, who laid no claim to being an outdoorsman. Clothes hung to dry on ropes strung between two wagons. There weren't many, and Dylan thought the pilgrims probably didn't have all that much of anything.

By the time Jackson's buggy came to a stop near the north wagon, the pilgrims had gathered and stood silently waiting. Their faces were drawn with worry. Even the children were subdued and quiet.

Jackson strode to the group, whacking his quirt against his leg as he walked. The people backed up a step or two and stood closer together. A tall blonde woman in a long loose dress stood out front. Dylan wondered if these farmers let women run their business for them.

Jackson came to a spraddle-legged stop before the woman.

'Who are you?' she demanded.

'I represent the Aripaiva Land and Cattle Company,' Jackson declared. 'My people brought you here safe and sound. We've met our obligation.'

'You promised free land,' the woman said, demand still in her voice.

'There is free land for homesteading all over this country,' Jackson said. 'All you have to do is locate it.'

'Where do we homestead?' she demanded.

'Madam, we brought you here. Land must be obtained from the government by homestead or purchased from those who already own it.'

'We gave you money. You lead us to the land.'

'No, ma'am.' Jackson pulled a piece of paper from the inner pocket of his coat. 'Here is our contract,' he said, opening the folded document. 'It says the Arapaiva Land and Cattle Company will transport fifty-three men, women, and children to Alchesay County, and provide wagons and pulling stock at the rail siding at Sulphur Springs. Then the company was to guide your party to a campsite from which you could conduct your search for suitable land to homestead. That was our agreement, which is authenticated here by the mark of your leader.' Jackson squinted at the contract. 'I read the name under the mark as Jonathan Beckwith.' Jackson folded the paper up with a flourish and returned it to his coat pocket.

The woman looked confused. She turned to the older man who stood slightly behind her. He shrugged.

'Madam,' Jackson continued, 'our contract is complete. Aripaiva Land and Cattle Company has fulfilled its responsibility to you. Your future is now in your own hands.'

The camp was totally silent, except for the thin wail of a baby in one of the wagons.

From behind the rise above the camp came the rattle of harness and the sound of iron wagon-wheel rims and horseshoes striking stone. A driver hollered at his team, and a wagon with two outriders topped the hill. Nat Dylan immediately recognized Jared Carter astride a buckskin horse; his right palm went instinctively to the handle of his Remington.

CHAPTER EIGHT

When the gaggle of two wagons and half a dozen horsemen halted at the edge of the camp, Carter spoke first. 'Jackson, if you got nothing to add to helping these folks out, just ride on out.'

Then he turned to Nat Dylan.

'Dylan, I know you want me, and by rights it's about time we settled what's between us. But I'd take it kindly if you'd put off the shooting today. These women and children don't need to have bloodshed as the first thing they remember about their new home.'

Dylan looked at the children, most of them hanging to the skirts of their mothers, and after a little while he nodded and crossed his hands over his saddle horn.

'Thanks,' Carter said.

'These people have paid in full. Isn't that right, Jackson?'

'They did.'

'You're satisfied that your outfit has been fair and

aboveboard with them?'

'We did what our contract called for.'

'How do you expect them to make it through the winter? Here it is August. Nothing besides radishes will mature before the frost comes. Besides, right now, they have no land to farm.'

'They can homestead like everyone else.'

'I swear to God, Alton Jackson. You make me sick. Get out of here before I throw up all over your shiny boots.'

Jackson strode to his buggy and climbed onto the seat. He threw a poisoned glance at Dylan. 'Do your duty,' he said, but Dylan merely smiled and kept his hands crossed over the saddle horn.

'Damn people who don't do their jobs,' Jackson said to no one in particular, and flicked the reins at the fillies in the buggy's traces. They lunged against the traces and the buggy raised a cloud of dust as the team dashed up and over the hill. Wagonwheel cowboys followed at the gallop. At the top of the rise, Nat Dylan pulled Bronc to a stop. He sat there looking down on the sodbusters' camp. Finally he lifted a hand, then turned the roan to follow Jackson and his men.

Two days later, Bronc threw a shoe, and Dylan took him to the blacksmith shop on the corner of Third Avenue and Main Street for shoeing.

'What'll it be, Dylan?'

'Horse needs shoeing, Swan. Can you do it today?'

'Got me some good help now. You leave that

cayuse here, wander over to the Iron Skillet and have a bite of dinner, wander back and we'll have 'er done.'

'New help, eh?'

'Yep. Jared Carter brung him over yesterday. Said he knew the right end of a hammer. So I give him a little test, and let me tell you, that man can smith. Almost as good as me.'

'Where's he from?'

'Arkansas, he says, and before that, Wales. He's camping over by Levine Creek until them folks get settled, he says. Can't stand here jawing, Dylan. Got to hold up my end. Come on back in a couple of hours and that Bronc horse of yours will have four brand new shoes.' Swan shrugged his immense shoulders and ducked into the shop. Dylan tied Bronc at the end of the line of horses waiting to be shoed, and walked down Main toward River Street. Carter again, he thought. *No one moved a finger to help those sodbusters out, except for Carter, and whomever Carter asked for a favor, they gladly gave it.*

Dinner was over at the Iron Skillet; only the savory smell of good food remained. Nat Dylan took a seat at the corner table, sitting with his back to the inside wall.

Madge Pritcher came from the kitchen, fatigue showing around her eyes. 'Not much left, Nat,' she said, 'biscuits over chicken stew if you want. It's good and it's hot. That's what I'd eat.'

Dylan nodded. 'And coffee,' he said.

Madge smiled. 'You got it. Bring the mud out now?'

Dylan nodded again. 'What happened to beef and beans? Thought that was your standard dinner.'

'New cook. Town's a-growing. We get more people every day. Chilly Jakes is an old chuckwagon cook who knows meat and taters and beans, but now we got this woman that Jared Carter brought in. She's the one who made the biscuits on chicken stew thing. Almighty good.'

'Jared Carter?'

'He says the pilgrims out at Levine Creek won't make it through the winter without some cash money to buy food. I told him we couldn't pay much. He said a little cash was a hell of a lot more than none at all, that's what he said.'

'I'll be damned.' Dylan shook his head. Why would a shootist who gunned down three men in Ouray, Colorado, be spending so much time helping people he didn't even know?

Then the memory of the day in Ouray came surging back: pushing through the people gathered to see the bodies, recognizing Shig and Miles and Dave, grotesque somehow in death; not anything like his brothers when they were alive. Dylan couldn't shed tears then and none came now, but he remembered the vow he'd made when he first heard the name Jared Carter. Aloud he said, 'Jared Carter. Someday we'll stand out in the street with guns in our hands, and only one of us will walk away.'

Dylan hadn't seen Madge set his coffee down, but he did sit up and take notice when she brought a large plate of chicken stew with biscuit dumplings.

He knew by the smell this meal would be one to remember. Whoever that new woman was back in the kitchen, she knew more than a little about cooking. Dylan dug into the food and wasn't disappointed.

He'd finished the stew and was on a second cup of coffee when Carmen Vasquez came in. She wore a split leather riding skirt, flowing white blouse, and short leather vest. Her black hair was pulled back severely into a bun at the nape of her neck. She wore a flat-crowned leather hat that dipped jauntily over one eye. Dylan sat with his mouth open, coffee cup raised halfway to his lips. He'd never seen any woman quite so beautiful.

Carmen smiled and came to his table. 'Good morning, Mr Dylan,' she said.

He was barely able to mumble a greeting in return.

'May I join you?'

Dylan started. He'd like nothing better. He stuttered. 'M-m-my, er, of course, Miss Vasquez.' He stood to pull out a chair for her.

'You are a kind man, Mr Dylan,' Carmen said as she took her seat.

'I was taught to honor women, miss. I do what I think is right.' Dylan regained a part of his power of speech.

Carmen smiled. 'That's not what I meant, Mr Dylan. I was speaking of your kindness in bringing the bodies of poor Juan and Ramirez home so their families could properly mourn them and bury them with honor and the blessings of the church.'

Dylan blushed. 'It seemed the right thing to do,' he managed to say.

Carmen put her hand on Dylan's arm. 'That is exactly why I say you are an honorable man,' she said, and looking into his eyes, she showed her brightest smile.

Dylan fiddled with his hat.

'Coffee, Carmen?' Madge stood by the table. Neither Dylan or Carmen had noticed her approach.

'Oh. Why yes, please, Madge, that would be delightful.'

'Refill for me, Madge,' Dylan said.

Neither Dylan nor Carmen said anything until the coffee had been served. 'Doughnuts if you want them,' Madge said.

'Not for me, thank you,' said Carmen. 'I eat more than enough sweet food as it is. Mr Dylan?'

Dylan dearly wanted one of the Iron Skillet's famous doughnuts, but he couldn't after Carmen refused. 'No thanks, Madge,' he said. He sipped at the coffee and wished for a doughnut.

'You didn't have to do that,' Carmen said in a quiet voice. 'I don't mind if you eat a doughnut and I do not.'

'Wouldn't be right,' Dylan said.

Carmen laughed. 'You see? I said you were an honorable man.'

Dylan found he could not look directly at Carmen. He stared down at his coffee cup. 'A man should be courteous to a woman,' he said. 'That's only right. Don't know if it has anything to do with honor.'

Carmen smiled and Dylan noticed her dimples for the first time. He couldn't get over how beautiful and regal this young woman was. He knew now why that English knight threw his coat over that puddle so the queen wouldn't have to step in the grime. He'd gladly do the same for Carmen.

'Please don't think me forward, Mr Dylan,' Carmen said. 'But I want you to know you are welcome at Rancho Vasquez at any time you wish to visit. Perhaps you would like to come soon so the families of the two unfortunates you brought to us can thank you properly. Would that be asking too much?'

'I reckon I could ride out. I know the way.'

'When can we expect you, Mr Dylan?'

Dylan didn't know what to say. He had no plans other than killing Jared Carter. He had no duties at the Wagonwheel. Still, he had no idea of how to answer her. He finally decided to ask her back. 'That all depends, Miss Carmen,' he said. 'It all depends on when you all are ready for me to arrive.'

'Tomorrow?' she asked. 'Two days from now? Perhaps you would like to come on Sunday. You could attend mass with the family and then eat to your heart's content from one of Emilia's famous Sunday dinners. Yes. I think that would be perfect. Can we expect you on Sunday, then?'

Dylan felt he could say nothing but, 'Of course. That will be fine, ma'am.'

'Now,' Carmen said. 'Tell me about yourself.'

'Me?'

'Yes. I would very much like to know why a man of your reputation is so honorable.'

'Reputation?'

'I have heard people say you are a killer.'

'I don't think I am a killer, though some men have died by my guns.'

'Tell me why you are not a killer,' Carmen said, her dark eyes boring into Dylan's blue ones.

'I have never killed a man who was not trying to kill me. There is a rule out there that says when someone tries to kill you, you are allowed to defend yourself to the death – yours or his.'

'Why then, are you hunting Jared Carter?'

Somehow Dylan didn't want to talk about Carter with her. She looked beautiful and wholesome, yet her questions were as if they'd come from a judge. She smiled, but he wasn't sure if there was something else behind the smile.

'Miss Carmen. I like your company. I like to sit and converse with you. I like your laugh. I like the way your eyes sparkle. What I don't like is all your questions.'

'Have you something to hide, then?' Carmen's face took on a hard, serious look.

'No.'

'Then tell me what it is about Carter. It seems to be eating you alive.'

Dylan took a deep breath. 'All right. When I was fifteen and still a schoolboy, a man drifted into our town. Before he drifted away, he shot my three older brothers dead.' Dylan pulled the Remington from

88

his holster and placed it on the table. 'This was my brother Shig's favorite six-gun. When I took it from him as he lay dead in the street, it was covered with blood and mud. I swore to find that drifter and kill him for my brothers. The town marshal said the drifter's name was Jared Carter.'

Carmen put her hand on his arm again. 'I'm so sorry you lost your brothers,' she said.

Dylan bowed his head. The tears he couldn't shed when his brothers died now threatened to overflow. His throat swelled, and he couldn't speak.

'So you know how the families of poor Ramirez and Juan feel. You truly know.' She paused for a long moment. 'Nat Dylan, man of honor, will you not do me one favor before you come out to our hacienda on Sunday?'

Dylan managed to nod.

'Consider the law you quoted to me, the one that makes you not a killer. Consider that law, and see how it applies to Jared Carter . . . please.' Carmen stood up. 'Thank you for the coffee, Mr Dylan. We'll expect you at Rancho Vasquez on Sunday morning.

CHAPTER NINE

Bronc had four new shoes when Dylan got back to the smithy. 'How much?' he asked the Swede.

'Two bucks for the shoes, four bits for the shoeing,' the blacksmith said.

Dylan handed him two cartwheels and a fifty-cent piece. 'If they last as long as the ones they replaced,' he said, 'your price is more than fair.'

'Customers keep coming,' Swan said with a big smile. 'My price must not be too far off.'

Dylan returned the smile. 'Could be that you're the only smith in town, too.'

'Oh, I reckon about half the ranches around have a blacksmith lean-to. Most good cowboys can shoe a horse and make a running iron,' Swan said. 'But more folks are moving into Longhorn, and they've got to come to me. I'm a happy man, Dylan. Just plain happy.'

A steam whistle sounded a long *whoo-whoo* to let all and sundry know the 4.40 p.m. was coming into the Longhorn station.

'See you around, Swan. Much obliged for the shoeing,' Dylan said, and swung up on Bronc.

'Those shoes will last you, Dylan. You won't be back soon, but if you stick around Longhorn, you'll be back.' Swan laughed from the bottom of his sizable belly.

Dylan lifted a hand and turned Bronc toward River street. He decided to have a drink at the Angus and think things over.

Three horses stood hipshot at the Angus hitching rail. Dylan almost changed his mind, but he did want a drink and he did want to have a think. He could take a bottle and sit at the corner table. No one would notice him then. He looped Bronc's reins over the rail twice. The horse knew enough to stay put. He walked through the double batwing doors into the long saloon. The plank bar ran along the east wall, backed by a big mirror, rows of brown, green, and clear bottles, and a wooden keg. Dylan knew the barman and the barman knew him. 'Turley's Mill, eh?' he said.

Dylan nodded and stood by the bar while the barkeep pulled a brown long-necked bottle from under the counter and gave it to Dylan along with a double shot glass. He took the bottle and glass and went to sit at the north-west corner table, ignoring the three men at a table in the center of the room. Still, he felt their eyes follow him.

'Hey, Ben,' said a bewhiskered man to the slim nervous-looking man on his right. 'Didn't see no bottle from under the counter when we ordered whiskey. What's that dude got that we ain't?'

'Lay off, Rolly. He's drinking peaceful,' the man called Ben said.

Rolly downed a shot and poured another from bottle with no label. 'Alcohol. Tobacco. Rattlesnake heads. Chili pepper. And they call this whiskey.'

The third man spoke. 'When you want to pay an eagle a bottle, you can drink Turley's Mill, asshole.'

'I like good whiskey, Jinks. Think that slicker over there would share?' Rolly looked at Dylan's bottle with lust in his eyes.

'Go ask him yourself,' Jinks said, scratching under the arm of his once-white shirt. 'He don't look too friendly to me.'

'He ain't very big,' Rolly said. 'Maybe I could just take that bottle away from him.'

'He might object,' said Ben.

'I'll be polite, real polite,' said Rolly. He downed another shot of house whiskey, scraped his chair back, and stood up on slightly unsteady legs. He wove his way to Dylan's table.

'Hey, dude, how about a drink?'

'I only drink with friends,' Dylan said. 'Go back to your friends before you get hurt.'

'Hurt? Me? You ain't big enough to squash a bug, much less hurt a grown man. Now how about a drink of that good whiskey?'

As Rolly reached for the bottle, Dylan stood up. In the half second it took for him to draw his Remington, Rolly was hardly able to register that Dylan had moved. Dylan let the Remington continue rising until the forward sight of the long revolver took Rolly under the jaw. As the big man clasped both hands to his bludgeoned face, Dylan brought the Remington around and laid the barrel under the rim of Rolly's hat so it hit him across the ear, smashing it to his skull. The big man dropped in his tracks, unconscious.

Dylan already held the Remington pointed at the man called Ben. 'I think your friend's been hurt. If you want to make anything of it, we can go at it now, or you can wait until he's awake and come out in the street. I don't hold to people forcing themselves on me. One man or three.'

Ben looked Dylan up and down. 'Where in the street?'

'You come out, you'll know.'

Ben nodded. 'We'll be out, and you'll be dead.'

'Your bullet's got to hit me before you can kill me.'

'I'm not known for missing what I shoot at,' Ben said.

Dylan smiled. 'We'll see,' he said. He picked up his glass of whiskey with his left hand and tossed it back.

'Later, gentlemen,' he said. He holstered the Remington, picked up the bottle and glass, and walked to the bar.

'Sorry to bother you, Fred. Be back another day.' He strode to the batwings and pushed through. He took Bronc and tied him to the hitching rail in front of the Monarch on Lee Street where he was less likely to get hit by a stray bullet. Then he walked across River Street and took a seat on the porch of the railway station.

He pulled the makings out of his breast pocket and rolled a smoke. The short cigarette in his lips, he struck a lucifer on the heel of his boot and lit up. The man called Rolly would not come to for some minutes yet, and he wouldn't be itching for a gunfight for a while after that. Jinks. That quiet man was the one to watch. He'd go first. Then Ben. Dylan would worry about Rolly after that. He smoked the coffin nail down to a nub and ground it out under his heel. He pulled the Remington from its holster and added a sixth bullet to its cylinder. He put it back. All he could do now was settle down and wait.

Dylan sat on the station porch seat with a foot up on the balustrade. He puffed at his Bull Durham cigarette absently, his hat pulled down over his eyes. The sun was getting low and would soon be an advantage for anyone coming from the west on River Street. Dylan doubted if the three drifters would have that much savvy, but they might.

Then a hunched-over man ran across the street between the Angus and the Monarch. He looked like Rolly. The dance was about to begin. Dylan stood, watching the batwings of the Angus. The running man disappeared behind the Monarch. He'd come around the corner onto River Street, and that would put the sun in his face. Dylan drew the Remington, twirled the cylinder, checked the action and the loads, and slipped it back into the holster. He walked down the station steps to street level, and took half a dozen paces, angling toward the Monarch.

A shout came from inside the Angus, 'God damn your soul to Hell!' Ben came crashing through the batwings with his revolver drawn.

'Here I am, Ben,' Dylan called and drew the Remington.

Ben's six-gun bellowed and splinters flew from the station porch. Dylan brought the Remington to bear as if he were pointing his finger and touched off a shot. The man called Ben crumpled where he stood, then rolled off the Angus's boardwalk into the street. He lay motionless.

Dylan could see neither Rolly nor Jinks. He took another step toward the Monarch. Then Rolly's Colt appeared at the corner of the saloon. 'I'll teach you to buffalo me, slicker,' he shouted and triggered a shot that went wide. Dylan ran quickly east along River Street. The moment he could see half of Rolly's body, he stopped, raised the Remington and shot Rolly through the ribs.

Where was Jinks? The most dangerous of the three in Dylan's estimation, and nowhere in sight.

Rolly was trying to raise his pistol for another shot. Dylan triggered the Remington and his bullet tore a hunk from the siding two inches above Rolly's head. Rolly hunkered down behind the boardwalk. Dylan shook his head. That shot through the ribs should have taken Rolly out.

The big man poked his head and his gun above the boardwalk, firing a shot that snapped past Dylan's ear. Dylan fired true, knocking a piece of Rolly's head out and sending a spray of blood up the side of the Monarch. The big man folded like a rag doll.

'All right, Jinks,' Dylan said just slightly louder than his normal voice. 'It's you and me.' Dylan put the Remington back in its holster. 'How good are you, moocher?'

Jinks stepped into the street from behind Hughes Hotel, his back to the sun. 'I'm good enough to take you, slicker.' Jinks drew, his hand a blur going to the Frontier Colt at his hip. Dylan matched Jinks's draw, smoothly bringing the Remington up and touching off the light trigger. Flame blossomed from Jinks's gun as Dylan's Remington roared. A bullet plowed into Dylan's side, knocking him to the ground. Jinks took Dylan's bullet in the joint of his right shoulder; his revolver dropped to the street. He went to his knees, scrabbling for the Colt with his left hand. Dylan grunted and turned onto his bleeding left side. He raised the Remington and carefully shot Jinks in the head. Jinks convulsively pulled the trigger of his Colt as he died, putting a bullet into the hard-packed surface of the street ten feet away. He fell forward on his face. Dylan's eyes closed. Blood pooled beneath him. His breathing got shallower and shallower. The color left his lips. So this is the way it was in Ouray, he thought vaguely. So this is the way my brothers died.

Far off, he heard someone say, 'He's still with us. Get Doc Richards. Quick.'

Then he knew nothing.

CHAPTER TEN

Dylan came to in a room that looked white and sanitary as a hospital. He was naked, except that his torso was wrapped in muslin from armpits to beltline. A white sheet covered the rest of him.

A small rotund woman bustled in through the door. 'So you're awake, then? How do you feel?'

Dylan croaked. 'Like I been slit from gullet to God knows where. Who are you?'

'Dolores Richards, Dr Richards's wife and the nurse in this house. Now, we've got laudanum if the pain is too intense. What do you say?'

'Perhaps a little.' Dylan's throat was almighty dry and his voice sounded like a rasp working on old oak.

'Just a moment then. The doctor will be in to see you later.'

'Doctor Richards?'

'Dr Ethan Richards. We moved our practice to Horsehead just over a year ago. But I'm talking too much. Let me get you some laudanum.' She bustled from the room and returned with a flat brown bottle full of milky white liquid and a big silver spoon.

'Turn your head a bit. That's a good boy.' She poured a spoonful and fed it to Dylan. Then another. 'That's enough for now,' she said. 'You'll feel better in a moment.'

Dylan lay back and closed his eyes. A soft cloud enveloped him, taking the pain away. He smiled, and went to sleep.

'The patient is awake, Doctor,' said Dolores when Dylan opened his eyes. He felt like he had a hangover, but he'd only had one drink of Turley's Mill. He frowned in concentration.

'Well, now, Nat Dylan. It's been some time since you helped me at the Wagonwheel. How are you feeling?' The doctor bent over to look at Dylan's eyes. 'Hmm. You look awake and sane,' he said.

'I feel like the morning after the night before,' Dylan croaked.

'Laudanum will do that to you. A laudanum hangover's worse than any induced by whiskey.'

Dylan ran his hand over the muslin binding his body. 'What have you done to me, Doc? You've got me wrapped up like one of those Egyptian things.'

'Let me explain,' said Dr Richards. 'You see, the bullet entered your body just below and to the left of your navel, travelled through your intestines, and exited to the left of your kidney. You were very fortunate. Gutshot people most often die, sooner or later. Peritonitis is the usual cause. Dr Goodfellow in Tombstone, however, has proved that abdominal wounds need not be fatal. Following Goodfellow's precedent, here's what I did, after administering ether to keep you from feeling pain.'

Dylan wasn't sure he wanted to hear a lecture on surgery, but the doctor plunged on.

'First thing,' he said, 'I disinfected the entire area with carbolic solution. Then I made an incision – that's a cut – along the left side of the entry wound, starting just below your ribs and ending two inches below the entry. Do you understand?'

'I understand that you split me wide open,' Dylan said.

'That I did, but for a purpose. You see, I had to pull your intestines – guts, that is – outside your body so I could see and repair any perforations, er, holes. There were three holes in the small intestine and a nick in the large one. I trimmed them and sutured, er, stitched them up, and before replacing them, I washed your abdominal cavity out thoroughly with boiled water I'd let cool to a tepid temperature. With luck, you'll have no infections. I replaced the gut and sewed up the incision. Then I repaired the exit hole in your back. Took three hours to do, but I dare say you'll be as good as new before long. For now, you must stay in bed.'

'I owe you, Doc,' Dylan said.

'How's the pain?'

'Not so bad under the wrapping but my head hurts something awful.'

'We'll fix that for you. Dolores!'

'Yes, Doctor.' Dolores bustled into the room.

'A cup of willow bark tea for Nat, if you will, my dear.'

'Right away.' She left to brew the concoction.

'I'll leave you then, young man. Oh, by the way, you've had visitors. The young lady from Rancho Vasquez came around, and so did Jared Carter. As you were, I couldn't let them in. I'm sure they'll come again.'

Dolores bustled into the room with a steaming cup in her hand. 'Drink this down, young man,' she commanded.

Dylan and the doctor exchanged glances.

'You'd best do what Dolores says, Dylan. After all, she is the boss in this house.' Dr Richards laughed.

'I reckon I'll need to sit up somehow,' Dylan said.

'You'll not be wanting to put a lot of stress on your abdomen yet,' the doctor said. 'Try rolling onto your right side. Can you hold the cup with your left hand?'

Dylan groaned and slowly turned onto his right side. Dolores walked around the bed and helped him hold the cup while he drank the contents. 'There,' she said when he had finished, 'that will clear up your headache shortly.'

'Feels better already, Mrs Richards. Thanks.' Dylan let himself gently down until he was lying on his back again.'

'Unfortunately, we'll have to keep you on a liquid diet for a few days, maybe a week. And I don't mean Turley's Mill. You can have broth, milk, water, and whatever else you want that doesn't have alcohol or solids in it. Dolores will watch over you and make sure you eat properly. We can't have great chunks of beef and potatoes trying to push their way through your lacerated intestines.' The doctor stepped to the door. 'Take care of the young man, Dolores, thank you. I'll be off to see Mrs Simmons. She's feeling too poorly to come in to see me it seems. Later, my dear.'

'Just call if you need something,' Dolores said. 'I'll be no farther than the kitchen.'

'Do me a favor, ma'am?'

'Of course.'

'Could you hang my gun rig on the headboard? I like to have it close to hand.'

Dolores scowled at him. 'No one is going to bring a weapon into this house, young man. You won't need yours.'

'I don't feel right when that Remington ain't near by,' Dylan said, 'if you please.'

Grumbling under her breath, Dolores left the room. When she returned, she had Dylan's gunbelt and big Remington revolver in her two hands, held as far away from her body as her arms could stretch. 'This is a doctor's residence,' she said. 'Not a house of destruction. I will not have you firing this pistol in my house.'

'Not except to save my life, Mrs Richards, or yours.'

'Hmph. Regardless. Here's your tool of destruction.'

Dylan almost smiled at her ire, then thought better of it. 'Just buckle the belt and hang it on the headboard, please,' he said. 'And thank you kindly. I'll call if I'm needing anything.'

Dolores huffed and whirled around and bustled

out the door, plainly upset to have a firearm visible in her home.

Dylan grunted and slithered across the bed until he could reach the Remington. He grasped the butt and pulled the heavy gun from its holster. He rolled onto his back again with the pistol in hand. He held the gun up where he could see it and turned it over to look at both sides. Usually the gun was clean enough to eat with. Now it was covered with dust from River Street. He checked the cylinder. One bullet. He'd come that close. He looked down the barrel. At least the dirt had not gotten inside the barrel. He opened the loading gate and pumped the ejector rod while turning the cylinder. Five empty brass shells plopped on to his chest. He clutched them in a handful and laid them next to his pillow, then slithered over to where he could reach the bullets in the belt. One at a time, he pulled a bullet from the belt and pushed it into the cylinder, clicked the cylinder around, then added another bullet. He'd never taken so long to reload his revolver, but then he'd never tried doing it with a 6-inch slash in his belly, either.

'Missus Richards,' he called.

'Just a moment.' Her voice came from some distance away. Then the click-clack of her shoes on the pine flooring. 'What is it, Mr Dylan?'

'Sorry to bother you, ma'am, but do you have an old rag about that I could use to wipe my Remington with?'

'Oh, I suppose so.' She whirled and click-clacked

back into the house. Moments later she came with two wiping rags and gun-cleaning paraphernalia in a box. 'You might as well do it up right. The moving will help you get your strength back.' She whirled and left.

Dylan wiped the pistol down. Put a spot of oil on a patch and used the rod to swab out the barrel. Removed the cylinder. Dumped all the bullets into one of the rags. Used the rod and patch to swab out the cylinder. Wiped each bullet and shoved it into the cylinder. Used a rag to wipe away all the road dust he could reach. He blew out the trigger and hammer mechanisms and wiped them where he could. He replaced the cylinder and wiped the entire gun one more time. Now he was as ready as his sliced and patched body would allow. He put the Remington back in its holster, placed all the cleaning equipment in the box along with the rags, and slid the box on to the sideboard. He sighed. A man doesn't like to go unarmed.

He noticed the headache was gone. He lifted his arms above his head. The incision complained at being stretched, but yesterday's pain was gone.

Dolores came bustling in with a large bowl of beef broth. 'There's lots of marrow in this broth,' she said. 'That'll help your body make up for all the blood it lost.'

'Smells delicious. How do I eat it?'

'I'll put it right here,' she said, placing the bowl of broth on the sideboard. 'Now, if you skiddle over to the side of the bed, you should be able to reach the bowl and feed yourself.' Dolores left, bustling as always.

Dylan found he could feed himself quite easily, and the hot broth seemed to give him strength. If he had some clothes, maybe he could get up. He'd always heard that moving about helps wounds heal.

'Mrs Richards,' he called.

'Moment.' She came in with a second bowl of broth. 'A growing boy like you would never be satisfied with just one bowl,' she said. 'There's more if you wish.'

'What I really need is some clothes,' Dylan said.

'Your underclothes are mended and washed,' Dolores said, 'but your suit is still at the Chinaman's. I imagine blood is difficult to remove. I just left the stains on your underthings.'

'Could I have the unmentionables please?'

'Certainly. You must feel much better. Now eat your broth.'

He did.

Three more days Dylan lived on beef broth. He used the chamber pot beneath the bed to piss in and his liquid diet meant he had no other business with the thing.

Jared Carter walked in as Dylan was finishing his breakfast broth. Automatically, Dylan reached for the Remington.

'Just wait up there, Nat. If you'd look, you'd see I ain't heeled.'

Dylan sat on the edge of the bed and glared. He was glad Dolores had found him a night shirt, or else he would have been in his underwear when Carter came wandering in. 'What do you want?' he asked, all his belligerence showing.

'Take it easy, Nat.'

'I made a vow to three dead brothers going on five years ago. They were killed by a drifter named Jared Carter and I vowed on their dead bodies to find that man and gun him down. Don't go telling me to take it easy!'

Carter just smiled. 'Seems to me you're not quite up to a gunfight with me right now, young 'un. Why don't we let it lay until you're fully recovered? You backed off when I was wounded and unarmed. I can do the same for you. Deal?'

Dylan sat silent for a long moment. What Carter said only made sense. 'Deal,' he said.

CHAPTER ELEVEN

'Sheriff Campbell wants to see you, Nat. Do you mind if he comes in?' Jared Carter indicated the door as he spoke.

Dylan instantly thought of the card shark in Jackson's Hole. Was there a warrant out for him? 'What does he want of me?' he asked.

'Better hear it from the horse's mouth,' Carter said. 'OK if I call him in?'

'I don't have any clothes,' Dylan said.

'He don't care. Besides, I think you'll like what he has to say.'

'Oh, yeah? Well . . . OK. Let him in.'

Carter went to the door. 'Sheriff? Come on in.' He opened the door wide to accommodate Jim Campbell's ample girth.

'Are you Nathaniel Dylan?' the big sheriff asked.

'I am.'

'I have a bank draft here for one thousand dollars. You have claim on the reward for the Blevins gang. Them three you shot out on the street was Jinks

Blevins, Ben Forie, and Rolly Lancaster. They're wanted dead or alive back in Colorado. Five hundred for Blevins, two-fifty each for the other two. I vouched for you and brung the draft. That all right?'

Dylan took a deep breath, ignoring the stretching of his incision. 'Yes, Sheriff, I'd say it was all right.'

'Here's your draft, then.' The sheriff handed the paper to Dylan.

All of a sudden, Nat Dylan held more than a year's cowpoke wages in his own hand. The draft was made out to Nathaniel Dylan and was drawn on Wells Fargo. Good as gold.

'I didn't know, Sheriff. They were merely ruffians who pushed a man that looked like a city slicker too far. I'm happy to get the draft.' He gave the sheriff a thin smile. He wondered if the dead gambler in Jackson's Hole had put a price on his own head.

'I've heard about you, Dylan. Know you're quick. So far, here in Longhorn, you've minded your own business. I know you killed a man up at Jackson's Hole, but there ain't no flyer out on you for that, at least not in Alchesay County. So rest easy, and don't spend the money all at once.' The sheriff clamped his hat on his head, turned on his heel, and strode from the room.

'Now there goes a real lawman,' Carter said. 'Never wore a star myself, but my brother Jason was marshal at Dry Lake where the Condor mine was found.'

'My brothers were law in Ouray, but didn't wear badges,' Dylan said, the taste bitter in his mouth.

'Pays to have a badge if you're gonna lay down the law,' Carter said.

Dylan said nothing. Here stood the man who gunned his brothers down and they were talking as free and easy as old friends. In fact, if Carter hadn't killed his brothers, Dylan might well like him, and might even respect him. Damn! Damn! Damn!

The broth on the sideboard was cold. Carter and Dylan were silent for what seemed like a long time.

'Someone seen you and Carmen Vasquez talking in the Iron Skillet the other day. Told me about it,' Carter said. 'She's a good woman, Nat. You be good to her.'

'I was taught to respect women,' Dylan said. 'I know there are some that don't deserve respect, but that's true with men, too. Don't worry about me and Miss Vasquez. She was just saying thanks for something I done the other day.'

Dylan looked Carter in the face for the first time since he came in. 'Speaking of the other day, is that hole I put in you healed up all right?'

'Getting there. Still got a scab or two, but they don't hinder me much. I been shot before. I know what to expect.'

'I don't. Doc cut an almighty hole in me, pulled out my guts, patched the holes in 'em, washed me all out inside, stuffed my innards back in, and sewed me up. Fixed the hole in the back, too, I guess.'

'Lucky you got shot in Longhorn where there's a top-notch doc.'

'No woofing.' This time Dylan smiled.

Carter put a finger to his hat. 'I'll be seeing you, Nat. You're looking good for a ranny that got shot from Hell to breakfast. Keep it up and we can have some Turley's Mill together at the Angus.'

'Carter . . . much obliged for bringing the sheriff over. But much as I'd like to, I can't drink with you. You're my sworn enemy, friendly though you might be. It wouldn't be right to drink with you.'

Carter touched a finger to his hat again. 'Sorry you feel that way,' he said with a rueful smile. 'I'll be moving along. Oh, that roan horse of yours is at the livery stable. He's eating corn. He may be frisky by the time you get out of here. Hope to see you out and about before long.'

'I will be, don't you fret.' Dylan lifted a hand in farewell.

Carter left, shutting the door behind him.

Dylan reached for the bank draft on the sideboard. A thousand dollars. He'd have to get a money belt. He'd never had that much money in his whole life. He wondered what other no-goods were wandering around with prices on their heads. Mostly they were wanted dead or alive, but some were alive only. Might be interesting to leaf through the wanted flyers at Sheriff Campbell's office.

Absentmindedly, he lifted a spoonful of broth to his mouth. It tasted all right but had a film of suet on it that would choke a horse. 'Mrs Richards,' he called.

She soon came bustling in.

'Sorry, ma'am, my broth's got cold while the

sheriff and Carter were here. Is it possible to heat it up?'

'I'll get some hot broth for you. There's a pot on the stove.' She picked up the bowl of cold broth, bustled out of the room, and came back in a few seconds, it seemed, with another bowl full of steaming broth. 'Now,' she said as she put the bowl on the sideboard. 'Today is your last day on plain beef broth. Dr Richards says to start you on oatmeal porridge in the morning and to give you mashed potatoes and gravy for dinner. At night, you'll get slumgullian stew, but without the meat. We'll have you healthy in days.'

Dolores turned, and then turned back. 'Oh,' she said. 'Your clothes have come back from the Chinaman's. We see how you are tomorrow. Perhaps you can get dressed and walk about.'

Dylan downed the broth. To tell the truth, conversation with the sheriff and Jared Carter had tired him out, but tomorrow, tomorrow he'd walk out of here. He snuggled down in the bed and dropped off to sleep.

He opened his eyes in the blue-gray of dusk. He stretched his arms above his head, yawning in satisfaction.

'You slept well, Nat Dylan. It is good to see that you are recovering well from that terrible gunshot wound.'

Dylan whipped his head around. Carmen sat in a chair near the window.

'What in . . . what are you doing here?'

'I have come to see an honorable man who shot down three vicious outlaws in the streets of Longhorn without so much as a thought of the danger to his own life,' she said, and gave Dylan a dazzling smile. 'Are you well?' she asked, her voice tinged with concern.

Dylan pulled the sheet up to his neck. 'I suppose I am as well as can be expected for a man with two holes in his body and three in his guts.'

Carmen's hand went to her mouth. 'Oh, my. But you are alive. You look as if you could climb Mount Baldy before sundown. Our doctor must be a magician.'

'No, I wouldn't say that, but he sure knows what he's doing.' Dylan remembered his Sunday invitation. 'Miss Carmen. I apologize, but I don't think I will be able to ride out to Rancho Vasquez on Sunday. Would it be all right if I came out some other day, next week Sunday maybe?'

'Of course, dear Nat. You come when you are able. We will do nothing special. You will merely join the family in celebrating the Sabbath day.'

Sabbath. Dylan had not been to church since Ouray. Even then he went because Miss Shoemeister was always at church on Sunday and he wanted to look good in her eyes. For a moment he wondered whatever happened to Rebecca Shoemeister.

'Is that all right?' Carmen sounded worried.

Dylan smiled. 'Fine. I'll ride out the first Sunday I can sit in the saddle.'

Her smile brightened. 'That's wonderful. It's so

111

good to see you are recovering. I was so worried.'

'Don't worry about a no-good drifter like me. I don't even have a place to sleep that I can call my own.' How true, he thought. Out of school for five years. Almost twenty-one. Nothing to show for it. He bowed his head. 'I guess I'd better start growing up,' he said.

Carmen got up from her chair and walked over to the bed. She touched his hair with a tentative hand. 'Do be careful. Do come to the rancho as soon as you can.' She leaned over and kissed him on the cheek. 'Be well, my honorable man.' She turned and hurried from the room.

Dylan's cheek burned far into the night. Through his supper of three bowls of broth. Through his ritual cleaning of the Remington. Through the picture of her face imprinted on his eyelids when he tried to sleep. When he woke in the morning, it still burned. He wondered if it would ever stop.

'Oatmeal porridge this morning, Mr Dylan,' Dolores said as she opened the curtains to let the morning sunshine in. 'Lovely day outside. Do you prefer milk and honey or just honey or do you like porridge as it is?'

Dylan rubbed at his gritty eyes. 'Milk and honey, please,' he said. Today he would sit up. More than that, he would dress and walk on his own two feet; he was determined.

When Dolores came back with the porridge, Dylan was sitting on the edge of the bed, triumph in his eyes. 'That's fine,' she said. 'I'll just slide this little side table over where you can eat comfortably.'

Oatmeal porridge had never tasted so good. The feeling of something thicker than water sliding down his throat was almost sensual. He ate four bowls full.

'My clothes, please,' he said to Dolores as she gathered up the dishes.

'Sorry. The doctor needs to look at your incisions and change the dressings before you do anything else. He'll be in momentarily.' She bustled from the room just as Dr Richards came in.

'Ah ha. Sitting up, are we? That's fine. Fine. Now. If you will just remain sitting, I will remove the bandage and we'll have a look at your wounds, how's that?'

Dylan nodded.

'Now then. Arms up.' Dr Richards undid the end of the muslin binding and unwrapped it from around Dylan's torso, rolling it into a cylinder shape as he went. A single pad covered the two wounds in front – the bullet hole and the incision. The doctor carefully peeled it down and off.

Dylan looked at his abdomen. A giant centipede with a maroon body and black legs was attached to his body, it seemed. The bullet hole was just a small line with three black stitches in it.

'Good. No suppuration. No pus. Dry and knitting well. Let me see your back now.' Again the doctor peeled the pad from the wound. 'Just like the front. No suppuration at all. Dry. You knit quickly, young man. I'll remove those stitches in three days, I believe. I'll know better when I examine you again.

Now, some salve.' He smeared an evil-smelling concoction on the wounds. 'Learned this salve from an old Cherokee medicine woman. Strange ingredients, but it works.' He placed a pad on the front wounds. 'Now, if you'd hold this pad on until I get the muslin wrapper on.' Dylan gingerly held the pad to his body. The doctor deftly applied a pad to the back wound, held the end of the muslin over the pad, and rewrapped Dylan's torso. 'There. Nothing more for three days. You're looking very well, young Mr Dylan. Much better than I expected. Congratulations.'

The doctor strode out as Dolores appeared with Dylan's clothes. 'Do you really want to do this, Nat?' She put the clothing on a chair.

He nodded.

'Do you need any help? Here. Use these slippers for now. When you recover more, you'll be able to pull on your boots.'

'I need to do it all myself, ma'am. Thank you anyway.'

'Your choice,' she said, and bustled from the room.

Dylan struggled into his clothes. He found that the muslin wrap kept him from fastening the top button on his trousers and he had to let his leather belt out a notch. He shoved his bare feet into the leather house slippers and carefully stood up. The wounds stretched and pulled, but were not unduly painful if he hunched a bit. Slowly he walked to the door, the slippers scrubbing along the pine flooring as he went. As his body loosened up, Dylan's heart filled with something he could only call joy, a wonderful sense of pleasure at being alive and happiness that he could walk and talk and would soon be whole.

CHAPTER TWELVE

Alton Jackson pulled up the fillies with a hard jerk on the reins. He left the buggy standing in front of the doctor's house, looped a lead rope over the hitching rail to keep the team in place, and strode up the path and onto the porch. He knocked on the front door.

After a moment, he heard the swish of petticoats and the doctor's wife opened the door. 'Colonel Jackson,' she said. 'What may we do for you?'

'I understand young Nat Dylan is here,' he said.

'He is, and he's doing very well, too. Up and around scarcely a week after that terrible man's bullet perforated his intestines. Mr Dylan is doing very well indeed.'

'May I speak to him?'

'Certainly. This way, please.' Dolores led the way to Dylan's room. 'Visitor, Mr Dylan,' she called, rapping on the door.

'Come in.'

Dolores opened the door for Jackson to enter.

Dylan sat on the edge of the bed, fully dressed with

his feet encased in leather slippers.

'Well, young Nat Dylan. I see you are on your feet again.' Jackson smirked. 'It would seem that even paid gunmen get shot. Perhaps you were shooting at the wrong men.'

Dylan reached back with his left hand to grasp the handle of his Remington. He drew the gun from its holster, deftly transferred it to his right hand, and cocked the big spur hammer. He pointed the Remington at the Colonel's midriff, and spoke in a quiet voice. 'Would you like to find out what it feels like to be gut shot, Mr Jackson?'

Jackson took a step back. 'Why would you want to point that awful weapon at me? I've done nothing wrong. In fact, I merely came to tell you that your month is over and you are no longer employed at the Wagonwheel. Where would you like me to deliver your possibles?'

Dylan smiled and lowered the gun to his lap. 'Mrs Richards,' he called.

A moment later, Dolores bustled into the room. 'You called, Mr Dylan?'

'Mr Jackson just informed me that I have been relieved of my duties at the Wagonwheel, that ranch without cattle or visible means of support, and wants to know where to deliver my things. Would it be all right to keep them in this room until I move somewhere else?'

'Certainly, Mr Dylan.' She turned on Jackson. 'And you, sir, haven't a drop of human kindness running in your veins, or else you would not throw this young man out in the street when he is suffering as he is.'

Jackson tipped his hat. 'Dylan knew the terms of his employment. He'll have no argument, I'll wager.' He looked at Dylan.

Dylan nodded. 'That's right Mrs Richards. Mr Jackson hired me for a month, and that month is up. He has no call to keep me on. That's all right, ma'am. I don't particularly like working for men like him anyway.'

'Well, if you say so.' Dolores faced the Wagonwheel owner. 'Please bring Mr Dylan's things to us. We will keep them safe until he has other accommodations. Thank you. Will that be all?'

'Yes. With your permission, ma'am, I'll be leaving.'

'Please.'

Jackson strode quickly from the doctor's residence, untied his team, and whipped them into a gallop back toward the Wagonwheel, raising a roostertail of dust on the way.

'Frenchy!' he shouted as he handed the buggy over to Robby to lead to the barn.

'I'll be right there, boss.' The voice came from the direction of the bunkhouse.

Jackson strode toward the front porch, whacking his quirt against his leg in frustration. 'Damn! Damn! Damn!' He mounted the steps, threw open the door, and clomped into the front room. The best thing for frustration was a healthy drink, he decided. A bottle of excellent rye whiskey stood with his other liquors in the cabinet. He grabbed the bottle and poured two fingers of rye into a large glass. A quick gulp put half the whiskey into his stomach. The warmth spread through his system, softening the mood of frustration and bringing back his usual sense of confidence.

'What do you need, boss?' Frenchy Durand stood at the door.

'You know young Dylan survived that gut shot. He's doing rather well.'

'Yeah, I heard. Little shit.'

'Did you also hear the Double Diamond has a herd gathered? They're holding the cattle in Benbow meadow until a cattle train can be brought in. I really would prefer that Milo Willard not be able to pay his note.'

Frenchy showed one of his nasty smiles. 'If someone were to take that herd through Devil's Gate and down the De Soto Trail, chances are he could get a decent price in Mexico.'

'Rustling is a hanging offence, Frenchy. If the herd were well scattered and maybe some of them rimrocked off the Lockwood Rim. Willard would miss his due date.'

'How about Dylan. Want him outta the way?'

'I'm beginning to think he and Jared Carter are cut of the same cloth.'

'You paid Dylan to get rid of Carter. He couldn't. Or didn't. I can. How about I go after Dylan first and then take Carter, or the other way around if that's the way things work out. How much would that be worth to you, boss?'

Jackson thought for a moment. 'A thousand dollars and 10 per cent of the Wagonwheel,' he said.

One of Jackson's boys delivered Dylan's possibles to the doctor's house just before sundown. A quick check showed Dylan everything was there, even the two extra boxes of .45 shells he'd bought on Wagonwheel credit at Solomon's the day before he got shot.

'Doc,' Dylan said when Dr Richards came in to check on him. 'I don't like being cooped up in a single room with a window right over my head. If it's all the same with you, I'll pack my stuff and get a room at the Hughes, or maybe board somewhere. Do you know of anyone with an extra room for a quiet boarder?'

Dr Richards chuckled. 'You're quiet, Nat, but that revolver of yours speaks almighty loud.'

'Only when it has to.'

'If you must move, go to the Hughes. It's not far, and you can walk up here for check-ups when you need to. Have you had a stool yet?'

'I prefer chairs.'

'No. No. A bowel movement. A shit, in gross terms.'

'Not yet.'

'Should come soon with all the food Dolores is stuffing into you. Don't eat any meat just yet. Drink a lot of coffee or milk or any liquid that doesn't contain alcohol. Let see if we can't get a stool out of you by tomorrow.'

'Still prefer chairs,' Dylan said, deadpan.

'Not where this stool will come from, you won't,' Dr Richards said, and laughed out loud. 'You are getting humorous, young man. You must feel quite well.'

'I do. I think I'll try to pull on my socks and boots and take a stroll before supper.'

'That's fine. You do that, but make it a short walk. Dolores doesn't like to serve supper too late.' With that, the doctor left Dylan to struggle with his socks and boots.

What felt like half an hour to get the boots on actually came closer to ten minutes. Dylan found it easier to stand with his ankles supported by the flat-heeled boots. He reached for the Remington and the gunbelt, and buckled the rig around his waist. The holster settled easily behind his right hip, and Dylan felt like a whole man for the first time in more than a week.

He stood straight and took normal steps; he looked like a whole man. His tender abdomen wasn't ready for gut punches, but overall, Dylan felt amazingly well.

Pianos tinkled from both the Angus and the Monarch as Dylan stepped down from the doctor's porch. He walked slowly down Lee Street, which took him to River between the Angus and the Monarch. The temptation to continue with the bottle of Turley's Mill he'd left at the Angus hit him, but he swallowed the saliva and told himself the holes in his guts wouldn't take whiskey yet. He'd only been eating mushy food for a couple of days, and his guts had so far failed to prove they worked correctly. Still, as he walked, the stretching of his wounds lessened and he picked up the pace. By the time he got to the Angus, he strode like a man who'd never been close to a gunfight.

Dylan paused at the front door of the Angus, then passed by. He crossed River Street and stepped up onto the station porch. For a moment, he faced the Blevins gang again. He shook his head. He surveyed the dark length of River Street. Light spread from the Hughes Hotel and the Iron Skillet to the left, the Angus and the Monarch to the right, and the Gay Paree where River Street turned the corner and became Main. Solomon's Mercantile, on the corner of Grant Street and River, sat closed and dark. After a few moments surveying the scene where he's almost died, Dylan reversed his course and returned to Dr Richards's house down Lee Street.

He knocked on the front door. Dolores opened it. 'My goodness, Nat. You needn't knock. Just come on in. You are a patient here. Now, I have some nice soothing rice gruel with tiny bits of chicken in it. It's savored with salt and a tiny bit of black pepper. I hope you like it. Are you able to come to the dining room for your meal?'

'Of course, I'll be in directly.' Dylan went to his room to shed the Remington and hang the rig on the headboard post. He washed hands and face in the commode set up in the room, and went to the dining room to eat rice gruel. It did have tiny bits of chicken, so small Dylan had to examine the gruel closely to see them. Still, it tasted good and Dylan ate two large bowls of the sticky mass.

'You may have a cup of coffee if you wish, Nat.' Dolores held a pot of freshly brewed coffee and a thick earthenware mug.

'I'd kill for a cup of coffee,' he said, and laughed. 'Just a manner of speech, ma'am. Don't mind me.'

She held out the mug.

Dylan took it and waited impatiently as she filled it with dark coffee.

'Good Lord, that smells delicious!' Dylan couldn't help trying to take a sip of the steaming brew and managed to burn his tongue in the process.

'Patience, Nat. Patience.'

'Yes, ma'am.' Dylan set the mug down and began to stir the coffee with a spoon. He soon dared another sip, and savored the taste of well-roasted beans percolated to perfection. 'Mrs Richards, that's damn good coffee.'

'I thought you might like some. Shout if you want another cup. The doctor said you could have two and no more.'

'Thank you, ma'am. I just died and went to heaven.'

Dolores left Dylan to enjoy his coffee. Not long after he started on the second cup, he got the urge to make a stool. Out of habit, he went into his room to get the Remington and shoved it in his waistband. He picked up the coal-oil lantern hanging near the back door, made his way to the two-hole outhouse behind the main house, sat on the left-hand hole and let the 'stool' come.

Dr Richards sat in the front room when Dylan returned from the outhouse. 'How did things come out,' he asked.

'No pain. Seemed all right to me.'

'Good. Good. Take yourself off to bed. We'll take your stitches out in the morning.'

'Don't know that I'll sleep, but I'll go.'

Dylan went to his room and lit a lamp. The soft yellow light showed his bed covers turned down. The tightly closed window to the right of the headboard kept the night airs out. Three men were dead. The Wagonwheel had fired him. Jared Carter was out there somewhere. Suddenly, Dylan decided he'd not sleep in the bed. He pulled down the blind, shifted the bedclothes to a spot near the door to the front room, and lay down to sleep on the floor. For comfort, he laid the loaded Remington within easy reach.

A shotgun blast came in the dead of night. The windowpane shattered inward and the buckshot tore a ragged hole in the blind. The bed's mattress took a full load of shot; feathers floated in the air.

Dylan grabbed the Remington and cocked it, but there was nothing to shoot at. Maybe it was just as well he didn't shoot. Maybe now whoever took the shot would think him dead.

CHAPTER THIRTEEN

Shortly after daylight, Frenchy Durand rapped on the front door. One of the boys opened it. 'Where's the Boss?' Frenchy asked.

'Colonel Jackson has not come down yet, sir,' the boy said.

'Go tell him I'm here, boy.'

'Yes, sir. Immediately, sir.' The boy turned and ran up the stairs. Moments later, Alton Jackson came down, adjusting his suspenders on the way.

'I got the little bastard, I'm sure I did.' Frenchy said, his voice jubilant.

'What makes you so sure?'

'I shot him through the window of his bedroom at Doc Richards's place. I know how the bed lies. I got him.'

'Put someone to watching the Richards house. We'll soon know if he's truly dead.'

'OK, but I got him, I tell you. I did,' Frenchy said. 'You'll see.' He ran from the door to the bunkhouse. 'Rogers, hey, Rogers!' he hollered.

A few minutes later a horse and rider thundered from the Wagonwheel headquarters down Mine Road toward town. The rider didn't return until almost noon.

'Boss! Boss!' Rogers came pounding up the porch steps as Jackson sat down to dinner.

'Rogers,' he said, as the cowboy opened the door. 'I am engaged in dinner at the moment. Go report to Frenchy.'

Rogers skidded to a halt. He crumpled his hat in his hands. 'Well, yeah, I guess,' he stammered. 'Er, I'll go talk to Frenchy.' He fled.

The boys were clearing away the dishes and setting out the coffee when Frenchy Durand poked his head in the door. 'Now OK, boss?'

'Come in, come in. Coffee? Cigar?'

'Both, thanks.'

The two men lit short cigars and savored the aromatic smoke. 'What was Rogers's big news?' Jackson asked.

'The undertaker was at Doc Richards' place. Sheriff Campbell, too. And Jared Carter hung around. No sign of the doc. No sign of Dylan.'

'Does that make him dead?'

'No, but it means something serious.' Frenchy took a puff, then a sip from the fine china cup. 'Coffee cools too fast in these bitty thin cups,' he said.

'Priorities, Frenchy, priorities. We need to get the Double Diamond to default before anyone knows the note I hold is a forgery. I need to marry Carmen Vasquez; she's the sole heir to the Vasquez Grant.

126

Dylan must die or be dead. I have no idea how much he knows, but anything about the Wagonwheel is too much. Jared Carter noses into everything. Those pilgrims would have died off during the winter except for him. Now we can't bring in another bunch the same way. Finally, we need a herd. The Wagonwheel can't be a major ranch without a herd. Damn that Snyder Gang. You'd think they would keep their word.' Jackson knocked the ash off his cigar and jammed it into his mouth. He chewed at the tobacco in frustration. 'Now. Is Dylan dead, or is he not?'

'I'd say so, but still I don't know for certain.'

'Make certain. Get Jared Carter, too. Do I make myself clear?'

'I'll do it, Boss. You can count on me. Let me get a couple of riders.' Frenchy Durand drained the cup, made a face at the cool coffee, and left to round up some Wagonwheel gunhands.

'One of the Wagonwheel boys came snooping,' Jared Carter said. 'I imagine they're behind the shotgun blast through the window.'

The group gathered in the back room of Dr Richards's house included Nat Dylan, the doctor, Sheriff Campbell, undertaker Ebenezer Brown, and Jared Carter. Sheriff Campbell suggested that Dylan remain out of sight, that they call the undertaker over, and then sit back to see who came to the scene of the crime to find out if the assassination was successful. From what Jared Carter said, the finger pointed at the Wagonwheel.

'How long to I have to stay here?' Dylan said.

'Take it easy, Nat,' Carter replied. 'You get in too big a rush, you'll be dead.'

Dylan raised his mug, indicating to Dolores that he wanted a refill. 'If they find out I'm alive, they may try shooting it out,' he said. 'There's half a dozen gunnies at the Wagonwheel. What if they all come at once?'

'While we're doing nothing,' Doc Richards said. 'Why don't I remove the stitches from Nat's wounds. They're closed up and knitting well. Come over here, Nat. Sit up on this table and shed your shirt and underthing.'

Dylan sat, took off his shirt, unbuttoned his longjohns, and slipped his arms from the sleeves. Every eye but Dolores's watched.

The doctor unwrapped the muslin and set it aside. He removed the pads from over the wounds. He clipped the stitches, then pulled each out with a pair of tweezers. Dylan flinched with each stitch, but made no sound. Finished, the doctor swabbed each wound with a solution of carbolic.

'You look a hell of a lot better that I do,' Carter said. 'But then, all I had was an old Mexican medicine woman to repair me. Can't gripe about the job she did, though the wounds still pain me a bit now and then.'

'Thanks, Doc,' Dylan said, ignoring Carter.

'You should keep your torso wrapped for another week,' the doctor said. 'After that, it's entirely up to you.'

'OK, into the box,' Sheriff Campbell said, pointing at the coffin in the middle of the floor. 'It'll be sundown afore long and then we can sneak you into the Hughes; stick you in one of those itty-bitty rooms under the eaves.' The sheriff grinned. 'In with you.'

Dylan gingerly climbed into the pine box and shuddered as the undertaker nailed it closed. He didn't like tight places he couldn't get out of, but he had no choice but to trust the doctor, the sheriff, the undertaker, and Jared Carter, a man he should kill. He took a deep breath. Cracks in the pine of the coffin let in enough air for him to breath easily.

'Back your rig around, Eb,' the sheriff's voice said.

'Be right there,' the undertaker replied.

Then Dylan felt the coffin being hoisted and carried to the door. The four men juggling the coffin finally made it through the door, and Dylan thunked down on the bed of the undertaker's hearse-wagon. The door closed and the hearse rolled serenely down Lee Street toward River. Dylan caught the tinkle of pianos as the hearse passed between the Angus and the Monarch, taking a right onto River Street. It turned onto Washington Street and into the undertaker's yard. Someone lifted one end of the coffin and then the other, gradually moving it sideways onto a solid floor. Some rattling and banging, and the hearse rattled away behind the clopping of its horse's hoofs.

Silence.

The lid was nailed down. Dylan didn't have his

Remington to pound the lid off. He knew he should just relax and wait, but the closed darkness of the coffin smothered him. He forced himself to stay still. Trust them, he told himself. A difficult thing to do. He'd trusted no one but himself now for going on five years. Got to be a habit. Damn this dark box.

A tap.

Another.

He tapped back.

'You're on the dock at Eb's,' Carter's voice said. 'As soon as I've scouted around to see if anyone's lurking, we'll sneak over to the Hughes and up the back stairway.'

'I want my gun,' Dylan said.

'I've got it. Now give me time to have a look-see.'

The coffin didn't feel so tight after Carter left. Now Dylan knew the others were holding up their end of the plan. He sighed and tried to relax. Couldn't. His nerves could serve as fiddle strings.

About the time Dylan wanted to scratch his way out of the coffin with his fingernails, Carter returned. 'Can't see anyone,' he said. 'That doesn't mean no one's there. Are you ready to try a sneak?'

'Anything to get me out of this coffin. I'm beginning to feel dead.'

'Hold on.' Carter inserted a pry bar under the lid and gently levered it off the box. Dylan took a deep breath of the night air, even though he knew he shouldn't. Who knew what vapors and plagues might be out at night. Carter stuck out a hand. Dylan grabbed it and pulled himself to his feet. He stepped

130

out of the coffin, and Carter handed over his gun rig. 'Don't you go pulling that thing on me, now,' Carter said. 'We've got more important fish to catch.'

Dylan buckled the gunbelt around his waist. The familiar weight of the Remington against his back reassured him. He took the six-gun from its holster and checked the action and the loads. He added a sixth cartridge to the cylinder as the hammer had been resting on an empty. 'I'm ready,' he said in a low voice.

The two men crossed Washington Street, Carter in the lead. At the back of the Hughes, a stairway led to the second floor, flattened out in a landing, then climbed to the third.

'You go first,' Carter said at Dylan's ear. 'I'll be a step behind.' He drew his Colt .44, which was dulled with soot so it would not reflect any light. 'Your Remington's not lampblacked,' Carter whispered. 'Leave it in the holster unless there's shooting.'

The moment he nodded, Dylan knew he was a fool. Carter, who killed his three brothers, a step behind him with a drawn gun. *A shot in the dark. Nat Dylan falls dead. Who knows who did the killing?* Dylan shook himself and started up the stairs, his hand on the butt of the Remington.

The shot, when it came, plowed into the two-by-four stair railing, putting a splinter in Dylan's left hand. In the half second it took Dylan to draw, Carter fired two shots. Dylan dropped to a squat, Remington at the ready. A dark shadow moved. Dylan and Carter fired as one. The shadow threw its arms wide and crumpled to the ground. The sound of running boots, then a running horse; Carter holstered his Colt. 'That's probably it for now,' he said. 'Let's go have a look at the shooter.'

Dylan eared back the hammer of the Remington and turned toward Carter. With a slight movement, he could shoot Carter in the head and his brothers could rest in peace. He stared at Carter for a long moment, released the hammer of the Remington, and put the gun back in its holster. 'I reckon it's about time . . . to see who did the shooting.'

Carter turned his back to Dylan, who'd sworn to kill him, and led the way back down the stairs.

The dead man was Dick Rogers. Now Dylan knew for sure the Wagonwheel tried to kill him. 'I don't like getting shot at from ambush,' he said as he looked down at the dead man. 'I think killing should be done face to face. It's never a good thing for a man to die, even if he's shooting at you. What was the number of the room you got for me?'

'Thirty-four,' Carter replied. He held out the key. '*Cuidarte*, Nat. Right now we're both on the wanted list. They want you. They want me. I suggest we call off our day of reckoning until this Wagonwheel mess is cleared up. That all right with you?'

Carter thrust out his hand. After a moment, Dylan took the proffered hand. 'Until the Wagonwheel mess is cleaned up,' he said. 'Truce.'

CHAPTER FOURTEEN

'Damn it. We don't know a Wagonwheel rider pulled the trigger of that shotgun, and we don't know for sure that they fired at you last night.' Sheriff Campbell paced the floor, rubbing a hand through his thinning hair. 'Dick Rogers is dead, but he didn't kill anyone. So we can't just ride up to the Wagonwheel and arrest everybody for murder.'

'I know one Wagonwheel man who murdered,' said Dylan. 'I watched Frenchy Durand slaughter two Mexican sheepherders, one just a boy. Do you call killing Mexicans murder in this county?'

The sheriff fixed his pale blue eyes on Dylan. 'You saw him do it?'

'I did.'

'Why didn't you say that when you brought those bodies in?' The sheriff wore an accusing look on his face.

'I rode for the Wagonwheel then.'

'Goldamn misplaced sense of honor. Howsoever, now you'll swear in a court of law that Frenchy killed them?'

'I will.'

'Then I'll get an arrest warrant for him – what's his real name?'

'Desmond.'

'I'll get a warrant for the arrest of Desmond Durand for the murder of. . . .' The sheriff was writing at his desk.

'Ramirez and Juan,' Dylan said. 'I don't know their other names.'

'. . . two Mexican sheepherders known as Ramirez and Juan. Shouldn't take long. I oughta be back before noon.'

Sheriff Campbell returned with the arrest warrant as Madge began serving dinner to the group sitting at the center table in the Iron Skillet. 'Got a warrant for Durand,' he said. He pulled a slight, whip-leather-slim man forward. 'Deputy Morgan will come along.'

'Sit down and have some dinner, Jim, Buck. Can't serve warrants on empty stomachs. What'll you have?' said Doc Richards.

Campbell pulled up a chair and waved the deputy to another. Madge refilled cups of coffee around the table. 'Steak and fried potatoes for me, Madge,' he said.

'Same,' said Morgan.

'Jackson will have his guns ready,' Dylan said. 'No way he's going to let you walk in there and take away his biggest man. He's got one less rider with Rogers

134

gone, but there will be half a dozen including Jackson and Frenchy. Knowing what I know of the Wagonwheel, they'll be ready to fight.'

'We only got a warrant for Frenchy.'

'Still. . . .'

'I'll ride over with you, Sheriff, if you don't mind,' said Jared Carter. 'Never liked seeing a murderer get away.' He looked at Nat Dylan as he spoke.

'I should go, too,' Dylan said after a moment. 'I know the Wagonwheel better than any of you.'

'Glad to have you along,' Campbell said. He fished two badges from his vest pocket. 'Consider yourselves deputies,' he said, and passed the badges to Dylan and Carter. 'Be sure you're wearing those badges when we ride onto Wagonwheel land.'

While the sheriff and his deputy wolfed down steak and potatoes, chased with Madge's good coffee, Dylan walked to the livery stable and got some help saddling his roan. He found he could mount the horse on his own without too much pain from his healing wounds. He rode Bronc to the Iron Skillet, dismounted, and tied him to the hitching rail.

Dylan's gunbelt had its full complement of thirty-four .45 caliber center-fire cartridges and his Remington held five more at the moment. Thirty-nine shots if this turned into a drawn-out gun battle. He settled his short-brimmed hat on his head, adjusted the Remington in its holster, and strode into the Iron Skillet. He joined the men at the table for one last cup of coffee.

'Well, men, let's go serve that warrant. If Frenchy

comes peaceably, that's good. If they want to make a fight of it, let's be ready.' The sheriff pushed his chair back and stood up. Carter pinned his star on the pocket of his shirt; Dylan likewise, the first time he'd ever worn a badge of any kind. The four men paid for their meals and the sheriff led the way out the door.

They rode abreast down River Street, turning right onto Mine Road. The sheriff and Carter held Winchester rifles upright on their thighs. The deputy had a double-barreled 10-gauge Greener. Dylan rode with the reins in his left hand, his right resting on his thigh, ready to bring the Remington into play at any second.

The gate to the Wagonwheel property stood open as if in invitation.

'Ride easy,' the sheriff said. 'We only want Frenchy, if he'll come peaceable.'

The men spread out. Dylan to the left and slightly behind the sheriff. The deputy on the sheriff's right and nearly parallel, and Jared Carter wide to the right, .44-40 Winchester now laid across the saddle bow.

'Man with a rifle in the barn loft,' Dylan said in a low voice.

'Rifle behind the bunkhouse,' Carter said. 'Looks like he's laying down.'

'Comes to guns,' the sheriff said, 'watch for them kids. Don't want any of those boys hurt.'

'Kids can carry guns, sheriff,' Dylan said. 'One points a gun at me, he's dead.'

'Can't see any more men outside,' Carter said. 'Could be they're in the bunkhouse or the main house and plan to shoot through the windows.'

They rode into the front yard without a shot fired. 'Hello the house,' called Sheriff Campbell.

Alton Jackson stepped out from the front door. 'Gentlemen. To what do I owe the honor of this visit?'

The sheriff took a folded document from the inside pocket of his coat. 'I have a warrant for the arrest of one Desmond Durand, commonly known as Frenchy, for murder. Turn him over peacefully and we'll ride on. Resist and you personally, Mr Jackson, run the risk of arrest for obstructing an officer of the law.'

'You ain't gonna take me for doing in no Mexicans!' Frenchy's shout came from within the house. He smashed a window with the barrel of a rifle but pulled the trigger too quickly to hit anything.

Dylan palmed his Remington and gigged Bronc straight at the barn. As the man tried to settle his aim on Dylan and his charging horse, Dylan touched off the Remington. The first bullet struck the framing of the loft window, flinging splinters into the gunman's face. Dylan kept firing as quickly as he could thumb back the hammer. His fourth bullet glanced off the rifle stock and plunged into the man's chest. He dropped the Winchester and fell forward out the loft door.

The man lay crumpled on the ground, out of the

fight even if not dead. Dylan whirled Bronc to look for the rifleman by the bunkhouse. Apparently he'd trusted the gunman in the loft to get Dylan because he was firing at the men in the front yard. Dylan had only two cartridges left in the Remington. He reined Bronc to a stop, aimed carefully, and shot the rifleman in the back of the head. Two down. Maybe four to go.

As he ejected the spent brass and reloaded his Remington, Dylan took in the scene in front of the house. The sheriff's horse down. The deputy nowhere to be seen. Jared Carter behind the watering trough near the eastside fence. Desultory firing, both from the main house and from the bunkhouse. Dylan knew Frenchy was in the main house. With six new cartridges in his Remington, Dylan decided to stop the crossfire from the bunkhouse. He backed Bronc out of sight and dismounted. On his way to the bunkhouse, he checked the man he'd shot. Dead.

He paused at the door. Two people firing from inside. The door opened in, so he'd be facing the gunmen from his first step inside. With the Remington cocked and ready in his right hand, Dylan reached for the latch with his left. With his wounds, he was in no condition to crouch so he just opened the door and walked in.

A gunman he didn't recognize shot from the nearest window. As Dylan stepped in, the man started turning to bring his rifle to bear. Dylan triggered a shot that caught the man squarely in the forehead.

He dropped in a heap. The next gunman in line was Peters. Dylan thumbed the hammer back. 'What'll it be, Peters? You want to kill Carter, the man who sent help for you at Mill Valley Knoll? If you don't, just lay the rifle down.'

Peters laid his rifle on the nearest bunk and raised his hands. 'Didn't like doing this no how. Mind if I sit down?'

Dylan waved his gun.

Dan Jones lay in the far bunk, still unable to do anything but struggle to the outhouse on a pair of crudely made crutches. The bandage on his stump looked like it hadn't been changed since Doc Richards amputated his leg. Dylan made a mental note to tell the doctor.

'Give me your word you'll stay out of the fight,' Dylan said to Peters.

'You've got my word.'

'Just stay on the bunk, then.'

Peters nodded.

Dylan closed the door behind him as he left the bunkhouse. He heard the boom of a shotgun, but couldn't tell exactly from where it came. Deputy Morgan, no doubt.

Fitful rifle fire from the house seemed aimed at Carter behind the trough and the sheriff behind his dead horse. Dylan stepped away from the bunkhouse and walked toward the Wagonwheel ranch house. At about halfway, Carter shouted, 'Drop, Nat, drop!'

Without thinking, Dylan let his body drop as if he'd been clubbed. He heard the *whfft* of a bullet

139

passing over him and the roar of Carter's rifle, the spang of a bullet striking metal and a scream. Dylan rolled over with his Remington pointed at the barn. Ray Stanley sat spraddle-legged, his back against the side of the barn. Carter's bullet had skimmed down the rifle barrel, smashed into the casing, and splattered into Stanley's right arm, just above the wrist, shattering bone and plowing its way to his elbow. He rocked back and forth over his smashed arm, moaning.

Rifle fire chewed at the water trough, but the solid structure held, protecting Carter from the bullets.

Now it seemed only one man's gunfire came from the house. Had to be Frenchy. Alton Jackson squatted, huddled in the corner of the front porch. A man who hired others to do his killing, he now seemed only interested in keeping out of the line of fire.

The sheriff popped up to take a shot at the house and a bullet sliced through the top of his left shoulder. He dropped out of sight behind the horse.

'We've got you outnumbered, Frenchy,' Carter called. 'Me, Dylan, and Deputy Morgan against you. Give it up.'

'You ain't gonna take me alive!'

Dylan got to his feet, his wounds feeling as if maybe they'd been torn open again, but there didn't seem to be any blood.

Deputy Morgan came from the barn lugging a large tin can. He motioned Dylan over. 'You smoke?' he asked.

Dylan nodded.

'Got any lucifers?'

Dylan dug a small bundle from his shirt pocket, unrolled it and offered the matches to the deputy. He took one. 'This'll be enough,' he said.

The two men were out of Frenchy's line of sight. 'Come on,' Morgan said, angling around to the back door. Quietly opening the door, they found Jackson's boys huddled in the kitchen. 'You all had better get out of here,' Morgan whispered. 'I'm going to burn this house down.'

The boys scrambled for the door.

'Ronny? Tom? What's going on in there?'

The boys were already gone, running like scared deer for the safety of the wash where Dylan once practiced with his Remington.

The deputy quietly emptied the contents of the can on the kitchen floor, allowing it to spread across the entire room. 'Better back out,' he said to Dylan. 'Hold the door open.' Morgan struck the match against the side of the house and tossed it into the kitchen. With a little *whoomph*, the coal-oil caught fire. In minutes the whole back of the house was ablaze. Frenchy's only route for escape was the front door or a front window.

Dylan and the deputy worked their way behind the bunkhouse and around to its south side.

'The house is on fire, Frenchy,' Deputy Morgan shouted. 'The only chance you've got to stay alive is to come out with your hands high.'

'You sons of bitches!' Frenchy Durand came

141

charging through the front door, levering and firing his Winchester as fast as he could. He aimed at Carter's water trough, then the sheriff behind the horse. Deputy Morgan quietly stepped out from behind the protecting end of the bunkhouse and shot Frenchy with a double load of buckshot from his 10-gauge Greener shotgun. Frenchy flung his arms wide and fell back, unmoving.

Morgan reloaded the Greener. 'You watch Jackson,' he said, and slowly walked out to stand over Frenchy Durand. 'Shot dead while resisting arrest,' he said.

CHAPTER FIFTEEN

The Wagonwheel ranch house burned to the ground. Fortunately, the fire didn't spread to the barn or the bunkhouse. Nevertheless, Alton Jackson no longer had a headquarters. Jackson ruled his domain from a room at the Hughes Hotel. His 'boys' boarded with charitable folks around town.

Longhorn looked sleepy to the lone horseman. He crossed the Claro bridge and reined his lineback buckskin down Main Street toward the courthouse.

'Whoa, Buck,' he said to the lineback as he reached the building with SHERIFF painted on the window. He dismounted, looped the buckskin's reins over the hitching rail, and walked in the open door of the sheriff's office. 'You'll be Sheriff Campbell,' he said, extending a hand. 'I'm Ness Havelock, US Marshal out of Apache County, Arizona.'

Sheriff Campbell, his left arm in a sling, stood to shake the marshal's hand. 'Jim Campbell,' he said. 'Ness Havelock. I've heard songs about you and your Spanish wife. How you rescued her from that bald outlaw and all.'

Havelock laughed. 'Songs say a lot more than they mean most times,' he said, ignoring the sling.

'Anything we can help you with? Have a seat.' The sheriff waved at a chair.

'Could be,' Havelock said, sitting in the chair. 'Could be.'

'Just ask,' the sheriff said.

'Yes, well, sometime back we had a man come into our town from Texas,' he said. 'He had a big herd following him. He faked a lot of papers and tried to scare people into giving up their claims and moving on. In our town, he was known as Judge Harlow Wilson, an upstanding citizen who took in boys who'd lost their families. He went to jail for what he done in our town, having an upstanding rancher and one of his hands killed, but he managed to get a pardon.'

Havelock looked longingly at the coffee pot. 'That coffee fresh?' he asked. 'I been on that blasted buckskin's back for more hours than I want to count. I'd admire a cup of coffee.'

'Sorry I didn't offer you one right off,' Campbell said. He took a cup from a peg by the stove, poured it full, and handed it to Havelock.

'To get back to my story,' the marshal said, sipping at the coffee. 'My, that's fine. Strong enough to eat horseshoes. Mighty fine.

'I got word from the Pinkertons that Judge Wilson was up to some of his old tricks. Forging notes on property, taking on little boys and being pretty rough on them, promising herds of cattle that never materialize, and the like. Only now I understand he says he's a colonel. Have you heard of anyone matching that description?'

'We have us a colonel in town, Marshal. One who had four young boys on his spread, waiting on him hand and foot. He's got a note on the Double Diamond. Don't know if it's a forgery. His men murdered a couple of Mexican sheepherders the other week and the man who did the killing died while resisting arrest not long ago.'

'Is this colonel still in town?'

'He lives at the Hughes Hotel at the moment.'

'Would you be so kind as to introduce me to him?' Havelock removed his badge and slipped it into a vest pocket.

'Surely.'

Havelock stood and drank down the coffee. 'Mighty fine,' he said again. 'No time like the present. Let's go meet your colonel.'

Dylan sat at the back corner table savoring a second cup of Madge's fine coffee when two horses pulled up in front of the Iron Skillet. One was Sheriff Campbell's new piebald bay, the other was a big lineback buckskin that Dylan had never seen before. The piebald had the sheriff's blocky form in its saddle, but the buckskin's rider was tall and slim with jet black hair, black eyes, and a dark complexion. The man wore a gray shirt, gray striped California pants, and a gray flat-crowned plainsman's hat.

There was something familiar about the stranger, but Dylan couldn't place just what. The two men dismounted and strode toward the entrance of the Iron Skillet.

Other than Dylan, only three customers sat in the restaurant. In the far corner opposite Dylan's table sat Alton Jackson, and two Flying M cowboys wolfed steak and spuds at the center table.

Sheriff Campbell came in and walked directly to Jackson's table. 'Good day, Colonel Jackson,' he said.

Jackson looked nonplussed by the cordial greeting. He glanced at the arm in the sling. Perhaps he remembered that only a few days before, Sheriff Campbell had exchanged bullets with Wagonwheel riders. 'Er, good day, Sheriff. Is there something you want of me?'

'Isn't that note you hold on the Double Diamond about due?'

Jackson smiled. 'It is, Sheriff. Day after tomorrow, to be exact.'

'Could I take a look at that note?'

Jackson extracted a leather wallet from his inside coat pocket. 'Certainly,' he said, his voice confident. But when he handed the paper to Campbell, his hand trembled.

'How does this look to you?' Campbell said, turning to the man who had come in unnoticed behind him.

The man took the note. 'Up to your usual tricks, eh, Jackson? Or should I say Wilson?'

Jackson narrowed his eyes to inspect the stranger.

'Havelock? Ness Havelock?' He sounded incredulous.

Dylan had not recognized Havelock, perhaps because back then he'd been riding the outlaw trail as wild and unpredictable as any gun-quick in the country. Now he looked like, well, like a lawman.

'That's right, Wilson. Ness Havelock. US Marshal Ness Havelock. I'm here to say you're under arrest for forgery and swindling. You and I are going to take a long ride, all the way to San Antonio. I'll keep this note, by the way.' Havelock folded the note and slid it into a breast pocket. He also brought out his star-in-a-circle badge and pinned it in place. 'Get what you can carry on a horse – you do have a horse?'

Jackson-Wilson nodded.

'Get what you can carry on a horse. You'll spend the night in one of Sheriff Campbell's cells. We'll leave in the morning. Sheriff, would you go with Mr Wilson to his room so he won't get any ideas about escape? I'll get myself a bite to eat.'

'Come on, Wilson,' the sheriff said. 'Milo will be glad to know he doesn't have to pay off that note to you.' He took the despondent Wilson by the arm and led him into the Hughes.

Havelock took an empty table.

'What'll it be, Marshal?' Madge asked.

'Coffee now, please. Steak and onions with lots of pepper. Can you do that?'

'Right away,' Madge said and hurried into the kitchen.

Havelock glanced at the two Flying M hands, who had ignored the goings-on with Wilson, then looked

147

at Dylan and looked again. Madge came in with a mug of coffee and set it down by Havelock. He picked the mug up, stood, and walked to Dylan's table. 'Hello, Nat Dylan. Long time no see. How have you been? May I sit with you?'

Dylan smiled. 'When I was a young duffer, I knew a rider named Johnny Havelock. You any relation?'

'Knew that boy myself,' Havelock said. 'He rode the Outlaw Trail from Jackson's Hole to Nogales and all the stops in between. Then he met a pretty little girl in Arizona. She turned his name into Ness and him into a rancher at the RP Connected. Now the Johnny you knew is Ness Havelock, US Marshal.'

'Ness Havelock. Does have a certain ring to it,' Dylan chuckled.

'And you, Nat. What brings you to a town like Longhorn?'

'Looking for my brother's killer.'

'Find him?'

'I did.'

'Did you call him out?'

'Not yet.'

Havelock sipped at his coffee. 'Why not?'

'I found out he's a lot better man than me.' Dylan stared out the window.

'How so?'

Nat Dylan talked with Ness Havelock as the marshal ate steak and onions and drank three cups of coffee. He told Havelock everything he'd seen Carter do, about the Wagonwheel men at Mill Valley Knoll, the pilgrims at Levine Creek . . . and finally he

said, 'And just last week, Marshal, he saved my life.'
Dylan explained the Wagonwheel fight to Havelock.
'He could have let Stanley shoot me dead,' Dylan
said, 'But he didn't. He shouted for me to drop. I
did, and he shot Stanley. I set out to kill Jared Carter;
now I owe him my life.'

'Sounds like you're between a rock and a brick
wall,' Havelock said. 'Let me tell you my experience.
When it comes down to the bare-ass bottom, do
what's right. Sometimes you have to think hard about
the right and the wrong of things, but do what you
know is right, and you'll be better off.'

'Yeah. Easy to say. Tough as hell to do.'

'But you can, Nat. You can.'

Dylan's throat closed. He couldn't say anything, so
he nodded. Then nodded again.

'Marshal?' The sheriff was at the door. Havelock
looked up. 'Shall I just take Wilson over to the jail, or
do you want to come along?'

'I'll be there in a minute,' Havelock said, and
turned back to Dylan. 'Do what's right, Nat, and
you'll never regret a day of your life.' He smiled, then
walked out to ride with the sheriff and the
despondent Wilson back to the county jail.

Dylan signaled Madge for another cup of coffee.
He had some serious thinking to do, and no one
could think without a cup of good coffee.

The Flying M hands left, so Dylan was the only
customer in the Iron Skillet. He sat hunched over the
table with both hands cradling his coffee mug. Do
what is right. What the hell was right when a man

149

killed all three of your brothers? How much did he do for forgiveness? Was there such a thing as forgiveness for killing? For a moment, Dylan remembered the Blevins gang. Men with prices on their heads. Did they have little brothers? Wives? Sisters? What would they think of Nat Dylan?

Dylan left half a cup of coffee and fifty cents on the table and went looking for Jared Carter.

CHAPTER SIXTEEN

Dylan couldn't find Carter. He'd never discovered where Carter lived. He wasn't in the Monarch or the Angus. Dr Richards hadn't seen him. Madge said he'd not been in for breakfast. His horse wasn't at the livery. 'But I seen him crossing the Claro bridge. Looked headed for Mud Flats,' the livery wrangler said. Nobody from Longhorn went to Mud Flats. That town was for Mexicans. That's where the buffalo soldiers from Camp Taylor spent their sparse pay.

Nevertheless, Carter could not be found in Longhorn, so Dylan saddled Bronc and turned the roan's head toward the cluster of adobes across the river. The town had another name in Spanish, but all in Longhorn called it Mud Flats.

No boardwalks in Mud Flats. Dylan figured most of the squat adobe structures had dirt floors. One adobe wore the word CANTINA painted on its side in peeling whitewash. Dylan had been off alcohol for more that two weeks now, but he'd drink if that brought information. He reined Bronc in at the rickety hitch rail and dismounted.

Inside, the cantina was dark with tiny windows set high in the walls and little tables scattered willy-nilly around the room. A lone patron sat far in the back. Dylan peered at the customer, a large man hunched over his drink.

A Mexican in white shirt and calf-length white pants came from the back room. '*Sí, señor?*' he said.

'Whiskey?' Dylan said.

'*Perdon,* no. *Tambien quiere beber el mezcal?*'

'Mezcal? *Sí.* OK. Mezcal it is.'

The man disappeared into the back and returned with a cloudy bottle of clear liquid, a small basket of quartered limes, and a dish of salt. Dylan took a seat against the wall and the man put the liquor, limes, and salt on the table before him. Dylan sat for a moment, not knowing quite what to do.

'*Perdon,*' said a voice from the other table. 'May I instruct you about the mezcal?'

Dylan looked up and recognized the speaker from the day the big Mexican rode escort to Carmen Vasquez when she came to the Wagonwheel. 'I'm Nat Dylan,' he said.

'Raoul Rodriquez. I have heard of your honorable character from Señorita Vasquez. Thank you for bringing us the bodies of poor Ramirez and young Juan.'

'You ride for Rancho Vasquez?'

'In a manner of speech. The Don once did me a great favor.'

'What do I do with the lime and the salt?'

Rodriguez poured a glass half full of clear liquor. 'Now, lick your finger like this. Then touch the wetted finger to the salt. Once more, lick the salt from your finger, take a mouthful of mezcal, then squeeze lime juice into your mouth as you swallow. *Sí.* Is very pleasant, no?' Rodriquez laughed.

The potent liquor spread like wildfire through Dylan's system. He knew he could not drink much without losing his faculties. He set the glass down.

'You do not like the mezcal?' Rodriguez was now sitting across from Dylan.

'It is very powerful. I must keep my wits about me.'

Again Rodriguez laughed. 'Why are you so careful this day, Nat Dylan, when so recently you were wounded, and fought with the bad men at Wagonwheel before you were completely mended? Is it not a day to celebrate. Fair and sunny. And you and I, we are alive.' Rodriguez tossed back his own mezcal.

'I wondered if Jared Carter might be in Mud Flats. Do you know?'

'Indeed he is here, my friend. He comes to *esta aldea* quite often, I think.'

'Where is he?'

'Drink the rest of your mezcal. I will show you.'

'I'd rather not. I must keep my head about me.'

'As you wish. Leave twenty-five cents for the drink, please.'

Dylan left two bits on the table and followed Rodriguez out of the cantina into the bright sunshine.

'We go,' Rodriguez said. He mounted his paint stallion and waited while Dylan got up on Bronc. Dylan felt a jolt of pride in his mount when he saw Bronc stood shoulder to shoulder with the stallion. The horses could have been brothers except for the coloring. Rodriguez's paint walked west along the dusty road that served Mud Flats for a main street. The jumble of adobes thinned and Dylan could see thin smoke away in the west. Sunrise, the Mormon town, he reckoned. The two horsemen passed the last adobe hut. To the left, atop a small rise, another adobe was under construction. Dylan could make out three people working on the structure. He rode closer.

Dylan recognized Carter from some distance off. He was tromping around in a puddle of mud. A young woman kept throwing handfuls of straw under his feet as he tromped back and forth, the mud coming nearly halfway up his calves.

Closer, Dylan realized the woman was Carmen. His heart jolted, then withered at the smile she flashed at Carter as he tromped about in the mud. Dylan's face turned into an expressionless mask.

'*Buenos dias,*' Rodriguez called as they got closer. 'How goes the building?'

Carter looked relieved at an excuse to quit stomping.

'Jared!' Carmen said. 'The adobe is not yet ready to put into the forms. Please walk around a little more.'

Heaving a sigh, Carter started stomping again.

'This way,' Rodriguez said. He dismounted and ground-tied the paint. Dylan did likewise. Together, they walked to where a young man in a dark brown robe, which was cinched about his waist with a bit of rope. He trowelled mud onto the adobe bricks already in the wall, smoothed the mixture out, then plopped a new brick onto the wet mud.

'*Buenos dias, padre,*' Rodriguez said.

The priest turned. 'Good day, Señor Rodriguez,' he said with a broad smile. 'Have you come to help with God's work?'

'Alas, no, Father. I bring a man who seeks Señor Carter. This is Nat Dylan. Señor Dylan, this is Father Pedro Benefico. He builds a church for *la aldea.*'

'For anyone and everyone who wishes respite from the cares of the world, Señor Rodriguez. Everyone is welcome.' The young priest smiled.

'The mud's ready for the forms, Padre,' Carter called.

'A young man to see you, Jared,' the priest said.

'I see him,' Carter replied. He walked over to the horsemen in his bare feet. 'Raoul. Nat. Nice day, eh?'

'Sun's out anyway,' Dylan said.

'What is it, Nat?' Carter's voice took on an edge.

'I reckon the time has come, Carter. Time for you and me to settle our problem. You're a good man, I've seen that. But my brothers are dead at your hand. I can't let that pass by. I'll be at the holding pens in two hours. If you're not there, I'll come hunting you.' Dylan reined Bronc around to leave. Carmen Vasquez stood by the mud pit, her hands over her mouth and tears in her eyes. Dylan rode by without a word.

In his hotel room, Dylan carefully cleaned the Remington. The bullets he'd pushed from the cylinder, he wiped and pushed into the loops on his gunbelt. He brushed his best black coat and got a clean white shirt from a hanger on the wall. The Chinaman had done a good job. The shirt was white as alabaster. He took his best black trousers from another hanger, again admiring the Chinaman's work. He stepped into the trousers and buttoned a pair of dove-gray suspenders on to hold them up. He carefully tied a cravat of pearl-gray silk around his neck. Clean socks with no holes. Wellington boots polished to a mirror shine. Black frock coat. Gray short-brimmed hat set on his head four-square. Dylan buckled on his gunbelt, which he had saddle-soaped and buffed to a shine that nearly matched his boots. He drew the Remington from its holster, checked the mechanisms, twirled the cylinder, and replaced the gun. He cleared the tail of the coat, putting it behind the gun. Suddenly he drew. Not half a second lapsed from the time his hand began to move until the Remington was in position to shoot. The gun felt light in his hand. He was ready. Ready as he'd ever be.

Dylan descended the stairs of the Hughes Hotel and left his key with the clerk. He led Bronc past the hitching rail so he could mount from the boardwalk without having to walk in the dust of the street.

At the holding pens, Dylan tied Bronc off to the side, well away from the chance of any stray bullets. He had no idea where Carter would come from, only that he would come.

Carter appeared from the corner of the jailhouse. He'd not changed clothes and mud still streaked his breeches. The gunbelt around his waist showed care and the Colt .44 in the rig glinted with a slight sheen of gun oil. Carter, too, had come for business.

Carter stopped about fifty paces from Dylan. 'We don't have to do this, Nat,' he said.

'You think I'll walk away? Do you think I spent the past five years hunting you just to walk away?'

'Nat.' There was almost a pleading in Carter's voice.

'Do you really think you can draw faster and shoot straighter than me? Do you really think I practiced day in and day out, shooting up a box or two of bullets a day just to walk away?'

'Nat. Listen to me.'

'Time for listening is gone.' Dylan shoved the tail of his frock coat behind the Remington so its handle was ready. 'I'm coming to you, Carter. You draw when you're ready.' Dylan started walking toward Carter, not in slow measured steps but quickly and surely.

Carter reached for his gun.

Dylan snaked the Remington from its holster, at least a quarter of a second faster than Carter. The Remington came into line. Dylan squeezed the trigger. The big hammer fell on an empty chamber. He'd left all of them empty.

157

Carter's eyes widened. His Colt fired. Dylan felt a mighty crash to his head.

For the second time in as many weeks, Dylan regained consciousness in the all-white room at Dr Richards's house. His eyes were still shut, but he could hear someone crying. His senses gradually cleared, and he felt drops of moisture on his upturned hand. Someone held the hand. He levered his eyelids open a crack. A dark mane of hair covered the woman's face as she wept over his unmoving hand.

'Carmen?' he whispered.

The sobbing slowed.

'Carmen?' he said a little louder.

The sobbing stopped and the head rose, exposing a face white with fear and eyes rimmed with red from crying. 'Nat? Nat Dylan. You terrible man. Are you still alive?'

Nat groaned. 'Perhaps. My head wants to split in two.'

'Oh, no!' Carmen jumped to her feet and fled from the room.

Moments later, Dr Richards rushed in. 'I say, lad. You're getting to be a regular customer.'

'I have a splitting headache.'

'Aha. Not surprising. You've a groove in your skull, too. Slight concussion, I should believe. Do you feel nauseous?'

'Nauseous?'

'Sick to your stomach.'

'No. Just the headache.'

'Willow bark tea coming up.' The doctor left the room shouting, 'Dolores!'

Carmen returned, with Jared Carter by the hand.

Dylan closed his eyes and turned his head away. The movement just about split his skull. He couldn't help a tiny groan.

'Nat!' Carmen wailed and broke into tears again.

'What kind of crazy man are you, Dylan? What kind of man calls another out to a shooting and comes with an empty gun?' Carter's voice carried an edge.

Gingerly, Dylan turned his head far enough to see Carter. 'Jared Carter, you're a much better man than me. You can do things for people that I can't even think of. And you've got Carmen. I saw how she looked at you when you were tromping adobe. Ness Havelock gave me some good advice. "Do what's right", he said, "and you'll never regret a day of your life." I believed him. I couldn't kill a better man, but honor said I had to call you out for killing my brothers. So now we're even. You saved my life. I saved yours. You're slower than cold tar with that Colt.'

'Of all the crazy dribble. I never heard the like. Carmen says you're a man of honor. I believe you are too. How many honorable men do you know? Nat Dylan, you're a rare man. And as far as me having Carmen, Jason and I were raised by her family; she's the only sister I have.'

Dylan turned to look at Carmen. 'Does that mean

I'm still invited to the rancho on Sunday?'

   'But of course,' Carmen said. 'Of course.'

   'Good. It's time I left the Killing Trail,' Dylan said.